MW00353113

BEYOND THE NORM

Feed Your Imagination

Anthology of Award-winning Short Stories

Copyright ©2019 by Scribes Valley Publishing Company. All rights reserved. Individual authors in this anthology retain copyright to their material and all rights revert to them. No part of this publication may be reproduced, stored in a retrieval system or transmitted in any form or by any means electronic, mechanical, photocopying, recording, or otherwise, except in the case of brief quotations embodied in critical articles or reviews, without the prior written permission of the publisher and individual author.

The stories in this anthology are works of fiction. Characters, names, places, and incidents are products of the authors' imagination or are used fictitiously.

ISBN-10: 0-9851833-9-X
ISBN-13: 978-0-9851833-9-4

DEDICATION

This anthology is dedicated to those who can see beyond the normal

To the authors featured in this book: Scribes Valley thanks you for your time, patience, trust, and talent.

CONTENTS

NORMAL IS A DIRTY WORD
A Foreword by David L. Repsher, editor

Normal. Common. Ordinary. Regular.

All dirty words when it comes to stories. Imaginations should recoil and gasp with horror at the mere mention of them. Nothing starves an imagination faster than an unimaginative story (pun totally intended).

Rest assured, the stories in this anthology are far from normal. They are beyond the normal. In fact, since normal is a dirty word, we must say that they are beyond the norm.

The authors presented in *Beyond the Norm* have discovered the secret of going past the barriers that squelch an imagination, the restrictions that cause boredom, and the limits that restrain a reader from becoming completely immersed in a story.

The variety of stories contained herein will amaze even the most demanding reader, so you should feel lucky that you've happened upon this collection of stories. And the first adventure starts as soon as you turn this page.

So, go ahead, turn the page, and feed your imagination as you take it beyond the norm. It will thank you for the trip.

FIRST PLACE

CONFETTI GIRL
©2019 by Mike Tuohy

Paula smirked when Todd passed her desk at a fast walk. "Don't miss your train."

Todd winced. "Just taking some mail to the post office." He displayed several large envelopes. "You have anything?"

Paula held up a postage due notice. "This came in the mail yesterday. You should be able to pick it up today. We also need some stamps." She stood and delivered the slip to Todd while making a *chooga-chooga* sound and pumping her arms in a locomotive mime. Todd pretended not to notice but he could feel his face was flushed as he stepped into the cool fall air. He was getting a little tired of the mockery from the young ladies at Harmony Landscape Design.

Todd walked slowly for the first block along Railroad Street. He paused and checked his watch before taking the left on Oak Street toward the post office and away from the tracks. The Crescent was running late. Probably delayed at Charlotte again. He resumed his journey at a normal pace. Upon reaching his destination, he heard the familiar pattern of the horn as the passenger train approached Flowery Branch. Two longs, a short and a long. Twelve minutes behind schedule. Not likely to make that up getting to Atlanta. Would Amtrak ever get their shit together?

Watching the morning passenger train go by was only part of the pleasure of dropping off the company mail. Just seeing Sharon made the trip worthwhile. The pretty little postal clerk worked the counter most mornings. Todd was glad to see her at the only open station. He wouldn't have to let people cut ahead of him to ensure getting served by his favorite.

Sharon smiled as Todd approached the counter. She'd already told him about her "invisible" braces and he could tell by the dark roots that her blonde hair came from a bottle. While Sharon was petite, he was stocky. Their children would be just right and his orthodontist uncle would surely give them a discount or financing if needed. Todd may not have been able to provide his mother the grandchildren she so desired in life, but she would still be pleased when she eventually got to meet them in Heaven.

"Good morning, Todd. Anything coming down the tracks I should know about?" She knew about Todd's enthusiasm for the iron horse, having seen him on a local TV feature about the nearby train museum where Todd volunteered. His four second appearance formed the basis of their conversations for some time. Unlike the office girls, Sharon's tone was not mocking and she often expressed an interest in trains. She still declined Todd's repeated offers for a tour.

"Since you ask, Sharon, I can tell you that the old Savannah and Atlanta steam engine 807 will be coming through Atlanta in a few weeks. It's an Alco 4-6-2 built in 1911 to serve on the Flagler extension. Has the original matching coal tender." Todd paused. He could tell he was losing her. "Anyway, it will be a real treat. Have you ever been on a steam excursion? I get a significant discount if you would like to join me."

Sharon sucked her teeth and shrugged apologetically. "My boyfriend's kinda going to be in town for the next month. He's coming to meet my folks and see if he can find a job."

Todd's jaw abruptly shut. A boyfriend. Of course, she had a boyfriend. Girls like her always have boyfriends. Burly guys with muscle cars but little understanding of what makes them go. No appreciation for real mechanical power. The smell of burning coal. The piercing blast of a steam whistle. The quickening chuff as the engine gained speed on rails of steel.

Sharon leaned to look around him. "Is that all today? There are other customers."

Todd refocused and slid the postage due notice across the counter. "This came yesterday."

"Right. I'll have to go fetch it." She signaled to a colleague who was opening another station. "I'll be right back, Chantelle."

The large black woman eyed Todd with a look that made him uncomfortable. Before Sharon started working there, he dealt with Chantelle almost exclusively. They had an amicable relationship, exchanging the usual pleasantries and laughing at the same corny things. He wanted to explain that his recent machinations in the queue were not an attempt to avoid her but it was just too awkward a topic to broach. Perhaps he could make a purchase from her to show that he had not turned into a bigot.

"Um, I could use a book of stamps."

Chantelle gave Todd a withering look. "You'll have to get those from your girlfriend Sharon. I got my own customers right now." She gestured to an elderly Asian man bearing a stack of small boxes. The man frowned at Todd as he shuffled forward.

A little shaken, Todd said nothing. At least he knew Chantelle understood his motives. Her referring to Sharon as his girlfriend made the recent news of her real boyfriend a little more painful. He might have to get familiar with the self-service system or take his business to the post office in Suwanee for a while. A bit of a drive, but it was right by the tracks.

Sharon returned with a large manila envelope. "It's from France. Would you look at that penmanship?"

Todd was already admiring the sweeps and curves. Seeing the company name in this flowing script put the current Harmony Landscape Design logo to shame. "And I thought calligraphy was a lost art."

Sharon looked confused then shrugged. "That'll be eighty-five cents. Anything else today?"

He would spare her the definition of calligraphy. Maybe her gear head boyfriend could explain it to her. "Just a sheet of stamps."

"The railroad commemoratives again?"

"Not today. Just the plain Old Glory design." Todd slid the company credit card through the reader. He really wanted those commemoratives but he did not feel like giving Paula an opening for more abuse. His day sucked enough already.

Todd took his time walking back to the office, stopping twice to admire the handwriting. It had to be a woman's hand. No doubt a beautiful woman. One with a naturally perfect smile, a delicious Parisian accent, hair the color God gave her and lips that begged kissing each time they parted. Perhaps she was applying for a position at Harmony. Might as well have a look. Ducking into the small municipal park along the way, he sat down on a bench, opened his vintage Union Pacific pocketknife and sliced the cellophane tape so neatly pressed across the flap.

Taking care not to bend the contents, Todd tilted them into his lap. The name, Claire Davies, hardly sounded French. The curriculum vitae explained. She was a British citizen in France teaching English until she found a job in her major field, landscape architecture. Behind the résumé was a small folder. When Todd opened it, he leaned back, his heart racing. She was the most stunning woman he's ever seen outside of a Victoria's Secret catalog. Wearing a sundress and a floppy beach hat, his life's new mission immediately became to help her achieve the dream of coming to America.

Paula was on the phone and squinting at her monitor when Todd walked in. Placing the postage stamps next to her keyboard, he headed straight to the copier and scanned Claire's documents, taking care to run the photograph at the highest resolution. Sending the images to his personal e-mail address, he put the original documents back in the envelope and ran a fresh piece of tape over his cut.

Paula hung up the phone and called out to him. "Was there something else? Looked like you had something in your hand. Is that your new train calendar?"

Her teasing didn't bother Todd much at first. He recalled his former crush on Paula and imagining how her lean physique and Nordic beauty would meld well with his more robust build and softer Irish facial features. Their offspring would be perfect. He abandoned these thoughts when she married an athletic tractor salesman of Cuban descent.

Todd had a new plan but it would require some finesse on his part plus a good bit of luck. Returning to the front, he handed Paula the re-sealed envelope. "Sorry. Thought it might be for me. It appears I was mistaken."

Paula studied the return address. "Brest, France?" She laughed. "Hope this isn't more of the boss's porn. He used to get it mailed here so his wife wouldn't see it."

Todd nodded. "I'm sure he gets enough via the Internet these days."

"You're probably right." Paula performed a dramatic shudder. "I've seen things he unintentionally saved to the server. At least, I hope it was unintentional."

Their low speech drew Candace from her office. Ever since it became plain that she and the boss were having an affair, she seemed to think every quiet conversation was about her. She was often right. "Anything for me?"

Paula shook her head. "Bills and junk mail."

Candace grabbed the manila envelope. "What's this?"

"Probably another résumé." Paula reached out and pinched a corner. "It's addressed to the boss man."

Candace yanked it free and gave Paula a condescending smile. "Well, he just made me personnel director. I believe I have the authority." She plucked a letter opener from Paula's desk.

"Sorry. I didn't get that memo." Paula turned back to her spreadsheet.

"He hasn't sent it out yet. Check your inbox in the morning."

Candace tugged the contents from the envelope. Todd cringed when she gasped and displayed the photograph. "Can you believe this? This girl wants a job here and she includes a picture like this?"

Paula looked up and laughed. "Maybe she thinks we're a high dollar escort service?"

Todd cleared his throat. "Actually, in Europe, it's common to include a photo with a résumé."

Candace glared at him and once more at the girl in the sundress. "Well, I don't care. It's not what we do in America and I think it's very unprofessional." Papers in hand, she rushed off to her office. Todd felt a twinge of sadness at the sound of each page passing through her shredder.

Paula whispered to him. "I guess our new personnel manager can't stand that kind of competition."

Todd shook his head. "Pity. The woman has a degree in Landscape Architecture from the University of Derby in England." Seeing Paula's quizzical expression, he stopped himself short.

"Did you look at it beforehand?"

"Oh, no. I just noticed it on her C.V. while Candace was showing you the photograph."

Paula smirked. "You should have been looking at the picture."

"Oh really? Is she pretty?" Todd bit his lip.

Paula held off responding as Candace marched by without making eye contact with either of them. She slammed the front door on her way out and peeled off as if leaving a bad date.

"Pretty ain't the word for it." Paula shut her computer down. "Five o'clock. My time's up. You coming?"

"I have to stay a little while and reinstall the CAD program on a couple of the computers."

"I thought you finished that yesterday."

"Erica didn't want me to update hers until she finished the River Oaks project. She's afraid of incompatibility issues."

Paula held up a scolding finger. "Just don't forget to lock the back door this time."

"Yes, ma'am." Todd went to his desk and opened his e-mail while Paula went through her usual routine of loading her purse, turning off lights and the usual last-minute bladder purge. When he could see her car exit the parking lot, he printed two copies of Claire's résumé. After locking the back door, he left one copy on the boss' desk chair and took the other home for further review.

Todd recognized the slender young woman standing by Paula's desk. She was even more captivating than the framed image on his dresser that he studied each evening for most of the past month. Hearing the voice that he only imagined now coming from her body was like hearing a beloved pet start to talk.

"Hello. I'm Claire."

That accent. She may as well have been Queen Elizabeth herself or any of a dozen British actresses he adored. He wanted to keep her talking just to hear her speak.

"I'm Todd. Todd Kelly. I work here. Here at Harmony. I do— various things." He regretted not having a proper job title. Mail boy. Technician. Errand runner. Each described what he did. Each was vital to the business. None sounded particularly impressive. He had a degree, for God's sake.

Paula intervened. "Todd has a degree in history and a devotion to steam locomotives. The present is not his long suit."

Claire tilted back her head and laughed. It sounded like music to Todd.

"Oh! I do love the old trains. In Britain, we have a marvelous system of railroads. I don't suppose you are familiar with Thomas the Tank Engine."

Todd was familiar but by no means a fan of something that so trivialized the technology but he was willing to play along for her. "Oh, yes. I volunteer at the railroad museum and take school kids on tours. The little ones often ask about—Thomas."

Claire tilted her head and gave an approving smile. "So, you don't mind working with the little blighters?"

Todd was silent as he considered the question. This woman

could only bear beautiful children. Well-behaved, polite and articulate. He and she owed it to the world to make that happen.

Noting Todd's silence, Paula jumped in once more. "You put him in the train zone again. It's hard to get him to snap out of it."

Before Todd could respond, Jeff Swenson, the president, founder and sole proprietor of Harmony Landscape Design emerged from his office. With hands on her shoulders, he guided the personnel director ahead of him. Candace managed a brief smile and nodded to Claire. "Candace. Welcome to Harmony."

Claire returned the smile and extended her hand.

Candace regarded the hand oddly and looked at the faces of those around her as if they were inquisitors and she a heretic. "I have to go!" She turned, walked quickly back to her office and slammed the door.

Jeff smiled sheepishly. "She's been under a lot of pressure lately."

Claire rocked her head. "We all have our bad days now and again."

A wail came from down the hall. Jeff shrugged. "Looks like Candace won't be joining us. We'd better get going. We have a reservation at Guido's. Hope you like Italian."

Claire nodded eagerly. "I love it. I spent a summer in Tuscany."

Paula clucked as she watched Jeff hold the passenger door of his Beamer for Claire, then close it like a chauffeur and jog around to the driver's side. "Good Lord! He looks like a teenager on prom night. Maybe I should call his wife and have her meet them there. I made the reservation for three."

Todd snorted. "I don't think that would be a good career move on your part."

Paula shook her head. "What I don't get is how he got her résumé. All mail goes through me."

"Maybe she e-mailed it to him."

Paula clicked her keyboard and studied the monitor. "Nothing on his company e-mail."

Something thumped loudly against Candace's door. Paula gave

Todd a questioning look. "Shoe?"

Todd shook his head. "That had some heft to it. More likely a stapler."

Paula pursed her lips and nodded. "Better steer clear of her for a while. I just couldn't believe how Claire just took it all in like she's seen it before."

"She probably has." Todd looked at his watch. "I'll be taking a long lunch. I need to go check on the restoration project over at the museum."

Paula smirked. "Good day for it. I have a feeling the boss will be taking a long one too." She picked up her purse. "As will I."

When Jeff assigned him to train Claire on the site design CAD system, Todd knew he had to play it cool with her and in front of the boss. Though Jeff never asked about the magical appearance of her résumé on his desk, Todd knew he was the most obvious culprit, not just in the boss's mind but in Candace's as well. She was very cold to Todd all that week when they passed in the halls. Jeff, however, seemed to smile at him just a little more than he used to.

The first twenty minutes together consisted mostly of Claire bemoaning the traffic, difficulties getting a work visa and her troubles finding an affordable car. Todd listened without interrupting. If chattiness was her way of masking nervousness, he didn't mind. He could listen to her for the rest of his life.

While the software updated, he managed a question. "So, how do you like it here so far?"

"Oh! Everybody's just been so lovely." She looked around and whispered so softly he could barely make out her words. "Almost everyone."

Todd pointed to his ear. "I'm sorry. I have a little presbycusis."

"At your age? You're far too young."

"We hammer a lot of metal over at the railroad museum workshop. We're restoring an old Baldwin 2-8-2 engine. The boiler is caked with lime." Todd stopped himself. He had seen that expression on Sharon's face before. He was doing it again.

Claire smiled doubtfully and continued just above a whisper. "It's just so amazing. Jeff paid for my airfare over here from France, set me up in a flat nearby, gave me an allowance for furnishings and I haven't made him any money yet. It's just overwhelming."

Todd shrugged. "So what's the problem?"

"Well, I don't think Candace likes me." Claire dropped back to a whisper but put her face close to Todd's. ear. "I think she hates me. I mean, she's the personnel manager but she evidently had not even read my résumé."

For weeks, Todd imagined the ideal scenario for confiding his role in Claire's hiring. This might be his best shot. "Candace shredded your résumé as soon as she saw it but I had already made a copy. I put it on Jeff's desk when she went home."

Paula's snort gave away her proximity. "I knew it had to be you."

Todd scowled. "I didn't know you were there, Paula."

"Obviously" Paula laughed. "I'm sure Jeff's wife would appreciate your help as much as Candace does."

Claire turned to her with a puzzled look. "He mentioned he was divorced, not that it matters to me, but what does Candace have to do with it?"

"Oh, sweetie! Hasn't anybody told you about Jeff and Candace?" Paula jabbed Todd's shoulder.

Claire's eyes widened. "Are they having an affair?"

"Well, they were until—" Todd could not find the words to finish.

Claire pointed to herself and looked from Todd to Paula. They each closed their eyes and nodded once.

"Well, I'll have you know that where I come from it's not unusual to have dinner with one's employer."

Paula tipped her hand in the air. "Three nights in a row is kind of pushing the norm. Was Candace at any of these?"

"Actually, no." Claire sat erect and spoke in a deliberate

haughty tone. "Well, he's going to be very disappointed when my fiancé shows up next week. He'll be here on holiday for a week to help me settle in and meet his parents. They live nearby."

Paula gave her a sly look. "So, you're not engaged to a Frenchman?"

The air seemed to seep out as Claire explained. "No. An American attached to the consulate in Paris. He has a year to go in his assignment after which he's coming to finish his J.D. at the University of Georgia. He has a passion for international law. We were to marry next fall. My having work here was supposed to help me gain citizenship." She choked up.

Paula put a hand on her shoulder. "So, you didn't mention your engagement to Jeff?"

"Didn't come up." Claire took a few breaths and composed herself. "Jeff was rambling on about some car he's planning to buy. He actually asked if I favored Lamborghini or Ferrari."

Paula nodded. "He's all about his image."

Claire shrugged. "I suppose. My father drives an old Morris Minor. I've never owned a car."

Todd was silent since the moment he heard the dreaded word. Fiancé? Of course, she has a fiancé. Girls like that always have fiancés. Handsome lawyers with luxury sedans and their faux leather upholstery, climate control and deluxe sound systems. Guys with no appreciation for the brass fixtures, diamond tucked velvet or varnished marquetry and parquetry of a robber baron's custom Pullman club car.

When the women went silent for some seconds, Todd became aware that they were staring at him. Between their half-whispering and his own thoughts, he missed most of their conversation. He did pick up that they mentioned some foreign cars. He decided to go with that. "I used to have a 1970 M.G.B. Fine piece of British engineering. Unfortunately, it was fairly easy to hot wire."

Claire stood and put a finger in his face. "You bastard! I could be back in France with my fiancé." She kept pace as Todd rolled backward in his chair. "Oh, sure! A chance at a career in America was tempting. That pig of a man will probably sack me next week and I will be stuck here with no job, no money and no fiancé."

When Todd's chair hit the wall, he stood up and looked around in panic. Claire turned away, sobbing, into Paula's open arms.

A distant whistle snapped Todd out of his paralysis. He glanced at his watch. The Savannah and Atlanta excursion train was right on time. If he wanted to see Engine 807 in all its chugging, smoking glory, he had five minutes to make a six-minute walk. He might make it at a run.

"If you ladies will excuse me, I have a train to catch." He squeezed past the embracing pair.

Passing through the front door, Todd could tell Claire had more invective to share. Gone was the sophisticated tone of the London aristocracy. She sounded more like a shrieking Bedlam inmate. Engine 807 drowned her out with two longs, a short and a long. The old steam whistles were so superior to the droning electric horns of the modern diesel engines. He could already smell the coal smoke in his mind.

About the author:

Born in New Jersey in 1954 (Eisenhower times) Mike moved to Georgia in 1965 (Maddox times) and has sopped up Southern culture ever since. A professional geologist working the environmental consulting rackets by day he chronicles the preposterous through flash fiction, short stories, novellas and a novel by night. A Pushcart Prize nominee, Mike has 26 published stories and his writing has been recognized in competitions in Canada, Ireland, England, Wales and the USA. A two-time finalist in The New Yorker Cartoon Caption Contest, he boasts nine words there. Mike lives quietly on the North Oconee River near Jefferson, Georgia.

SECOND PLACE

TANGLED LIMBS
©2019 by Andrew K. Clark

Mixon took the curve into the square much too fast. The tires of the small car squealed and Mixon had to swerve to the outside lane to avoid the trolly bus that was stopped straight ahead. The squares were designed for only one lane of traffic, of course, but the squares were wide enough for two lanes as long as there weren't too many parked cars. As he hit the straight away after passing the trolly, Mixon had to slam on his brakes to keep from hitting a couple in the crosswalk. The woman glared. Instinctively, Mixon put his arm up to brace the child on the seat beside him. The child slid forward on the leather; the seatbelt taut across his chest.

"You scare me," the child said in broken English.

With his window down, Mixon could hear the speaker booming from the trolly behind them.

"I don't know why that man is in such a hurry, but if you look off to your left you can see the Juliette Gordon Lowe House. Ms. Lowe founded the Girl Scouts right here in this house."

Mixon pushed the kid back against the seat. *You better be glad I'm in a hurry*, he thought. *If I don't get out of downtown, we can all go to hell and meet Ms. Lowe right now*. With the tourists clear, Mixon guns the gas, and the kid's head hits the back of the seat, just below the headrest. Mixon looked at his watch: twenty-two minutes left. Twenty-two fucking minutes.

Mixon sped around the square, picturing the roads in his mind, thinking through which path would have the least red lights. He pictured the grid in his head, the series of squares, of one-way streets in parallel, in opposing directions. If I can get to Price, he thought, I can make some time, then down to Oglethorpe. Only a few turns to the bridge over the river.

The kid was sobbing as he slid from side to side on the leather.

"It's inside *me* isn't it? Th' bad thing, it is, right?"

Mixon patted the child's head and brushed his dark bangs from his forehead. He looked over at the child, glancing back and forth from the road to the child's eyes, which filled with tears again.

"It's the bad thing. Ev'rybody knows about th' bad thing."

"There's nothing bad about you, young man."

Mixon forced a smile. The kid looked back at him, unconvinced. The kid's smart, Mixon thought, he knows. How could he not know?

Mixon made quick turns in succession, left then right, then left again. Traffic was light. That was good. He looked at his watch: nineteen minutes.

Mixon pictured the city streets in his head again. He was close to the Talmadge now. He could get the child over the river, away from people. He had initially thought to go through Garden City and over Alligator Alley into South Carolina. This would have added too much time. Plus, Garden City was too crowded. There was that one train that blocked the damned street, damn near every time Mixon went that way. Always when he was late. He pictured being stuck in traffic, cars all around, kids walking down the street when it happened right there, at the train. But what if it happened on the bridge, he thought? That could be bad. There won't be many cars on it this time of day, but still. No, he thought, I will get over the bridge and I will find a place to drop the kid. He looked over at the kid's golden cheeks. The boy had the kind of face you wanted to pet. He was about the same age as Emmie, he thought, and something about their faces were similar. They were at an age when boys and girls could be indistinguishable if you didn't have hair or clothes to clue you in.

The phone rang. It was Cate. Mixon hit the touch screen on the dash, sending her to voicemail. Just a couple more turns, then the bridge.

The tires complained as he banked the car hard turning onto Oglethorpe, the light just hitting red as he passed. A couple of red lights, past the bus depot. He would get the kid away from all the people, over the bridge, out into the country. He could drop the kid, and be back over the bridge in time.

Mixon saw a cop car down one of the side streets, its blue lights flashing. As his eyes panned upward, he noticed that the light of the police car was almost the same shade as the sky. The beauty of the day belied the darkness of what was about to happen, the horror in the seat beside him. Mixon looked over. The kid was staring at him.

The phone rang again. Mixon sent Cate to voice mail once more.

When they crossed MLK, traffic was stopped. Completely stopped.

"Come on, damnit!" Mixon yelled.

"You are angry with me," the boy said.

Mixon felt his face soften. He looked at the child. It isn't the kid's fault, he thought. The kid should be carrying some books home from school, should be kicking a soccer ball around the field. He should not be here in this car; he is not the evil one in this play.

The kid's eyes were big and doe-like, his pupils were dilated, nestled in the richest, darkest brown irises Mixon had ever seen. In the sunlight, he could see flecks of gold.

Fifteen minutes.

Mixon felt his chest tighten. He was determined to keep a brave face for the kid. He patted the kid on the head and, for a brief second, the boy's lips curled upward, threatening to form a smile.

"We are going over a big bridge soon," Mixon said. "You will be able to see a huge river, and lots of big boats, maybe a giant ship coming from the port. Do you want to see that?"

The boy nodded.

The port: another reason not to drive toward Garden City. There was no telling what could be spread through that port, maybe something that would make its way onto the ships. Maybe spread over the world in just a few days. My god, Mixon thought, this could be worse than what happened in Miami.

The phone rang again, the icon lighting up the dash. Traffic nudged along painfully slow.

Mixon punched the phone icon and Cate was over the speakers.

"Why do you keep ignoring my calls, mister?"

"Cate." Mixon fumbled with the buttons trying to take her off of speaker.

"I am at the Fresh Market," she went on, "and I am trying to see what you want me to pick up for the party."

"Cate, stop." Mixon pressed the glass buttons on his phone.

She was talking about coffee and about chocolate being on sale when he got the phone to his ear.

"Cate, stop. Please."

"Mixon?"

"Cate."

"Mixon, what is it?"

"Today was the pick-up. I've...I have one of the refugees."

"Oh my god, Mixon, you promised you wouldn't."

"How could I not, Cate, you know there is nothing else to be done. Who then?"

"Mixon!" her voice began to crack.

"Cate, listen to me. Everything is fine."

"Where are the others, there was a Carrier? You have the Carrier, is that what you're saying? Why you?"

"We were fine, everything was fine and then we got a group text."

"Oh my god."

Mixon looked over at the kid in the seat. Traffic began to move.

He was almost to the ramp heading up to the bridge.

"The Tribes?" Cate asked.

"Ishmael is taking credit," Mixon said.

"Oh my god, Mixon, you promised me, we talked about this, I told you not to do this, and you said, you said you wouldn't. Yes, I knew you would stay involved but this? Now this, now this Mixon? You promised."

"I know."

"Oh my god! How much time, how much time, Mixon?"

Mixon looked at his watch.

"Thirteen minutes, love. I am going to make it."

"Mixon, you *have* to make it. Oh my god. Where are you going?"

"We are headed over the Talmadge. I will find a road, I will pull off. I know a place. We will get deep in the woods. No one will..." Mixon looked at the child. "Everyone will be safe."

"Is it inside *me*?" the kid looked at him. A tear ran down his cheek.

"Everything is fine," Mixon said, juggling the phone and steering wheel to free a hand to pat the kid on the shoulder. "You're doing great!"

"Mixon," Cate started. "You will make it. You hear me?"

"I will make it."

"Where's my *oumi*?" the boy asked.

"Mixon, why didn't you tell me?"

"You would have lost it, but there's no other way, Cate. We can't just let them be taken. The others, they are all safe. We checked their stomachs. No sign. Nothing."

"Mixon."

"My *oumi*, have you seen her?" the boy was crying. "I don't want to be here."

By now they were on the bridge.

"Look," Mixon said, "Look out there on the river, do you see any boats, any big ships?"

The boy craned his neck.

"Mixon, oh my God," Cate cried in his ear.

Mixon hit the gas hard, swerving around a large eighteen-wheeler as they reached the midpoint of the bridge.

"Mixon." There was something different about her voice. Something he hadn't heard in her before, or hadn't recognized or remembered. Maybe it was the way she used to talk, the way she would say his name when they were first together. A kind of desperation, something that demanded he pull her in close. Maybe the way a child asks to share a blanket after a nightmare.

"I am coming home soon, love, I promise, and you can tell..." Mixon lost his voice and had to clear it. "You can tell Emmie I am coming."

"Who is Emmie?" The boy asked. "Is that your little baby, are you a papa?"

"I am a papa," Mixon agreed. "It's my daughter."

"Mixon." This time hearing his name sent a chill up his spine.

Mixon looked at his watch. Twelve minutes.

"Listen Cate, I have to go. I need to focus. We are going to get over the bridge. Away from downtown, away from the water. We have to get down one of the dirt roads, I know the place. I will get back. I promise."

"Goodbye, yes, yes, yes, drive. Yes, drive, be safe. You must get over there. You will call me when it is done? Drop him and run, you hear me?"

"Yes of course."

"You'll call me?"

"Yes, yes," he tried to make his voice firm, solid, maybe as much for himself as his wife.

"Goodbye," she said.

Mixon clicked the screen on his phone and threw it in the center console. He immediately picked it up and put it in his shirt pocket. In case he had to leave the car. They were on the backside of the bridge. Almost there, he thought.

As he did downtown, he pictured the roads that lay ahead, and he pictured one of the dirt roads that would wind away from

Highway 17, through the marsh, where once there were rice fields that divided Georgia from South Carolina.

"Where we going?" the boy asked.

"Oh, it's a beautiful place," Mixon again forced a smile. His face felt like plastic, as if one wrong move would make it crack.

"I want to eat food," the boy said, "but my stomach hurts."

"Oh, we will get food soon," Mixon said.

"It burns."

"I know, but that's OK, you're just hungry."

"It's the fire, isn't it? It's the devil's fire inside me. Right?"

"No, no, we are just going for a ride to show you some old trees, they are so beautiful you will not believe them." Mixon kept his voice level even though he was passing four cars in a double yellow lane.

"Then why did the other people take all the other kids away then? Why they not come to see trees?"

"Oh, they will come to see the trees."

Mixon patted the child's head again. He was at least nine, maybe ten, Mixon thought. He pictured the ugly scar up the center of the child's abdomen. Yes, he thought, I bet that burns.

"It's the fire, I know it. I heard the bad men say it when I was tied to the bed. They rubbed something on my belly, and it burned, like it burns now."

"We will get you some food," Mixon said.

"Why you lie to me?" the boy said.

The tires squealed and then the thumps from when you drive too close to the edge of the highway. Mixon steered quickly, putting the car in the middle of the highway. He squinted his eyes. Maybe two more roads, he thought. Then there is that long road that winds deep back on the marsh. He knew they were now a few miles from downtown. No one lived out here. This would work. This *had* to work. In Miami, the toxins fell over how many blocks? How many miles? He could not remember.

He looked down. Nine minutes.

None of the other children looked any different from this one,

Mixon thought. There was no harbinger, nothing to tip off the group until the text. Then the Rainbow Members running around jerking up the kids' shirts looking for the scar until they came to the boy and found it: a deep ridge that looked like raw hamburger meat. Ishmael looked at all those fresh faces, Mixon thought, and they chose this one. Mixon studied his face in quick glances as he drove. Why? Why him? Why Savannah?

Mixon turned onto the long dirt road and the car slid briefly. There was grass growing up between worn sandy tire tracks. Mixon floored the car and dirt filled the air behind them.

He looked back at the boy.

"What is your name?" he asked.

"I am called Hamal," the boy said. "Hamal means lamb, but my father says I am more lion than lamb!"

"Yes, you are," Mixon said, "I can see it in your eyes. So, I know you are brave."

"You think I am brave?" the boy asked.

Mixon took a curve and saw the marsh stretch out on either side of the car. The wild grass was bright green and at the edge of the horizon it seemed to mix effortlessly into the sky as if they were woven together.

"Yes, you are quite brave."

The boy smiled. The car jarred them both, as its tires hit deep ruts in the old road.

"We are going on a little adventure, you and I."

The boy's smile stayed in place. "We are?"

"Yes!"

Mixon pictured the tree where he would drop the boy, a huge oak that stood off by itself at the end of the road, a tree full of weeping Spanish moss that would catch the breeze like a postcard. It was a place Mixon had eaten lunch many days, when he wanted to get away from the world.

"We are going on an adventure, and I am going to take you to an ancient tree."

"A tree?"

"Yes," Mixon said. He looked at his watch. Six minutes. Enough time to drop the kid, turn the car around and drive away. He would make it to the road before it happened.

"I like adventure, and I like tree." The boy said.

"Well you'll love this tree," Mixon said. "I'm going to take you there and I'm going to drop you for a few minutes while I go get the others."

"Drop me?"

"Yes, I will let you sit under the tree, and I will go get the other children. We will all come back and go on an amazing adventure."

"You will leave me by myself?"

"Yes, but only for a minute."

"You cannot leave me," the boy stammered.

"Oh, it's only for a little while."

"No," the boy said.

Mixon saw the tree coming into view as they met a clearing. The land now narrowed to a strip containing just the borders of the road. Looking out of the car window, Mixon could now only see the water of the marsh beside the car. He steered carefully while trying to maintain his speed. Up ahead the tree almost looked like it sat on an island. There would be just enough room to turn the car around to make his escape, Mixon thought.

Five minutes.

"You can't leave me."

"But do you see the tree up ahead?"

The boy looked ahead. "It is a big tree," he said.

"It's a magical tree," Mixon said. "You'll feel its magic when you are sitting under it and I will bring all of the children back so that they can feel it too.

"You're leaving me to die."

"No."

"Because of the fire."

"No."

"That's why I feel sick," the boy said. "It's why you drive so fast."

"No, it's a magic tree."

They pulled up to the tree and Mixon slammed the car in reverse and turned the car to position it for departure. He got out of the car and ran around to the passenger side. As he reached the passenger side, he heard the automatic lock engage.

Fruitlessly, he tried the passenger door handle.

"Hamal!" he cried. "Open the door!"

The kid looked at him.

Mixon looked at his watch. Four minutes.

Mixon walked toward the road, away from the car. There might be enough time to make it if he ran. The cloud, he thought, would probably catch him.

Mixon looked up at the sky and back at the car.

He pictured Emmie. He thought of her on his lap. The way they would sit to watch a movie at Christmastime, the way her little feet perched on his. Cate had taken a picture of their feet like that last year. It was probably still on his phone.

"Hamal, I need the car to get the other children."

Hamal did not budge.

Mixon looked at the road. He took off running down the road away from the tree, away from the car. Away from the boy with the fire.

As he ran, he heard the car horn behind him. He looked back. Hamal was struggling to get out of the car through the driver's side. He got out and began running toward Mixon.

Mixon turned and ran away from the boy. How much distance could he create? How far could he get? Could he survive?

Behind him the boy yelled in Arabic and then in English.

"Why you no help me, why you leave me?"

Mixon stopped. He looked back at the boy.

"I am sorry about the fire, I am sorry they cut me open. I am sorry I come here."

Mixon looked at his watch. Two minutes. There was no time. There was no time left. Even if he were a sprinter, there's no way he could create enough distance, even if he had the car. The child was still coming toward him.

"They cut me," the boy said. "I didn't mean to sleep, they tell me to sleep."

Mixon began walking back toward the boy. He thought of Emmie. He thought of Cate. He instinctively patted his front pants pocket, looking for his phone. There might be enough time to call them to tell them he loved them. He would tell them how much he loved them. Except his phone was in the car. Maybe if he ran to get the phone, he could call them in time?

"You hate me," the boy said. "They tell me you hate me. All of you. You make war."

They were almost together.

One minute.

Mixon patted the boy on the head. He got down on his knees.

"You hate me?" the boy asked.

"No, I don't hate you." Mixon said. "I could never hate you."

"I am sorry," the boy said.

"No," Mixon said. "You know what I think?"

The boy looked at his feet.

"I think you're a very brave boy."

The boy raised his head slowly.

"I'm very proud of you for being so brave."

"I am brave?"

"Yes. And remember that adventure I told you about?"

"Yes?"

Mixon looked at his watch. "It's almost time."

"Almost time," the boy repeated.

"Yes," Mixon said. "Are you ready?"

The boy smiled.

"Yes. I am ready."

Mixon opened his arms and the boy stepped forward. Mixon hugged the boy close. Mixon looked over the boy's shoulder out over the marsh. He saw the place where the green grass and blue sky wove together and became one thing. He looked for the horizon, but could not find it.

About the author:

Andrew K. Clark is a writer, poet, and photographer whose work has appeared recently in *Out of Anonymity—The UCLA Writing Project*, *Good Juju*, and *NO:1 journals*. Main Street Rag Press will publish *Jesus in the Trailer*, his poetry collection, in the summer of 2019. He is the recipient of the Georgia Southern University Roy F. Powell Creative Writing Award. Andrew grew up in the small town of Alexander, North Carolina, outside of Asheville. His forthcoming book, *The Day Thief*, is a novel of magical realism set in 1920s Appalachia. An excerpt of the novel will appear in the February issue of *The Blue Mountain Review*.

THIRD PLACE

THE ORIOLE
©2019 by Catharine Leggett

An oriole in the tree. First one this season. She recorded the sighting in her book: *9:27 am, May 4th, 2017* (while dripping wet), and was certain, almost certain, pretty certain, this was the earliest sighting she'd ever had for the species, though she must leaf through her records for verification. Later. Not now. No time now. She'd make a note, add it to her growing pile of notes and lists. Would she ever get around to doing all that she had to do on the lists? Life was so fascinating, intriguing, and so many things needed investigating. If she'd lingered longer in the shower, and oh, it had been tempting—that hot water streaming down her body felt so soothing—she would have missed the little bird altogether. Wendy watched it flit from branch to branch then take off, bobbing up and down, up and down, on the air, then poof, it disappeared altogether.

She tightened the towel wrapped turban-style around her head and stared at the clock. So many things still to do before meeting Lisa, who would not want to be kept waiting for her beloved grilled cheese sandwich with smoked tomato soup, the lunch special at Avec Moi Café, served only from twelve to two, or until quantities lasted. Lisa would insist on arriving at noon because sometimes they ran out of soup. And where, Lisa would ask, did that leave the grilled cheese sandwich? Wendy liked the special, but if they switched it to tuna salad and chicken noodle soup, she could live with it. Not Lisa. She'd take it up with the waiter, ask to speak to the manager. "How come you're out so soon? I came here for the grilled cheese and smoked tomato soup and now you're out of soup? Grilled cheese doesn't pair with any other kinds of soup." Well, it did, but Wendy wouldn't argue with Lisa. And there's the other issue, too. Wendy watched her weight, but Lisa wouldn't make any sacrifices when it came to the grilled cheese, wouldn't consider settling for a salad. "Why shouldn't I have grilled cheese?" she asked. "I like it, so I should have it. How many times do we live?"

But that was Lisa, she'd never change. She was the same back when they were neighbours on Marvel Street, insistent on what she did and did *not* want. Getting what she wanted, when she wanted it, was not an issue with Wendy. Maybe that's why she went along with Lisa. First off, it was easier, but Wendy had a process for testing herself to see if she really wanted something. She'd ask, how would it change her life? Did she need it? She took, she liked to think, a rational approach which brought her to the discovery of whims versus needs. Total opposite of Lisa. But what did it matter to Wendy if she went along with Lisa's cravings? No sacrifices by her had been made if Lisa wanted, *needed*, a grilled cheese with tomato soup at Avec Moi. And their salads weren't half bad.

Wendy prided herself in her flexibility, probably the result of having to make do. Unlike Lisa, she had no rich relatives in her background, no executive husband with a comfortable pension and investments. She had more flexibility because she had no husband, no one to say *we must have this for dinner* or *no we can't watch that TV show*. That all stopped ten years ago when she gave Thomas the boot. Called him out on one of his lies. Sold the house on Marvel. Lisa still had Bill. He shadowed her when Wendy showed up at the house to pick her up—Lisa preferred not to drive—but he wasn't a talker, rarely said anything beyond a strangulated hello, or gave her a wave from the hall as he passed by the door while she waited for Lisa.

Five minutes. She'd give the oriole that length of time to make a return appearance and if it didn't, well then, *see you later Mr. Oriole. At a time that suits me.* In five minutes, she must start getting ready. Look how long it took her to prepare yesterday, the day the luncheon was originally planned. She ran around all morning, ironing a blouse, and putting a fresh crease in her slacks, and was just charging out the door when the phone rang. "What's it doing at your end of town?" Lisa asked. Wendy looked out into a dark, cloudy sky, but no rain. Lisa continued, "It's teeming here, absolutely teeming, and I don't want to go out in it."

"It's just rain," Wendy said. "Bring an umbrella."

"No," Lisa said. "This isn't umbrella rain. This is rain, rain. Like-something-out-of-a- movie rain. Monsoon rain. I'll wait and see if it lets up and call you back. No matter what, I'll call you back in an hour."

She hung up the phone and thought, now what? She'd planned her day around the lunch at Avec Moi, even started craving the grilled cheese since this was grilled cheese weather, spent forever pressing a razor-sharp crease in her slacks. After an hour and a half passed, she tried calling Lisa's cell. No answer. After two hours, she decided the luncheon wasn't going to happen and dashed off to the bank, and when she got back home, she realized she hadn't completed all her transactions. Some days she wondered where her head was. But still, it was so nice of the teller—Oh what was the young man's name? And so handsome! An unusual name, modern sounding. It would come to her sooner or later! He took such an interest in her, a personal interest. *Have you seen the new play at The Grand? Do you have Netflix?* He was so engaged by her, they talked together like a pair of old friends. The very reason she refused to go to an automatic teller, unless there was an after-hours emergency, of course. She wanted the human touch. Except, silly her, she got so caught up in their conversation that she forgot to do her money transfers and the deadline was looming.

Lisa phoned last night to apologize for standing her up—completely unintentional—and to describe the flood in her basement, the reason she forgot to call. "We had plumbers and emergency drainage people. It was a flood! A huge flood!" They rescheduled lunch for today. Lisa said, "I'm really going to need that grilled cheese and tomato soup! I need comforting now more than ever!"

Today, after lunch, after she'd dropped Lisa off, she'd go back to the bank. She'd go to the same teller, that handsome young man whose name she still can't remember—though it's coming, it's almost on the tip of her tongue—after the pleasantries they'd exchanged yesterday, the interest he'd shown in her, their conversation about so many topics—*Have you been to the new vegan restaurant on King Street?*—she didn't want to snub him and cause hurt feelings. Didn't want to imply in any way that their conversation meant nothing to her.

The doorbell rang, jarred her from her thoughts, as she stood at the patio door, staring at the tree, waiting for the little bird's return, wrapped in two towels, one around her head, the other around her body. She ran to the door and shouted from the other side, "Who is it?" No one answered. The doorbell rang again. "Just a minute!" She dashed upstairs to her bedroom, cast off a towel and threw on a housecoat. No time to put on anything else as whoever it was seemed to have their finger stuck on the doorbell. "Just a minute, for Pete's sake!" Some people could be so impatient! She ran back downstairs, shoved the towel out of her right eye, and opened the door to see a man yielding an electronic device and a clipboard. In the driveway, a service truck.

"Good morning, I'm from Home and Hearth, here to check your water heater."

"My water heater's fine, as far as I know. I haven't heard anything about this. I never called you."

He looked down at his clipboard. "Says here it needs checking. It's written right here. This a rental place?"

"Yes."

"Well, that's why, I imagine." His chubby fingers curled around the mechanical device he carried in his other hand. His fingers made her uncomfortable, slightly nauseous, though she'd no idea why, and yet she couldn't keep her eyes off them. "There's probably a system check going on in your townhouse complex. Notices were supposed to go out. Wouldn't be the first time I've heard of someone goofing, not sending them out. Anyway, I've got orders to check it out." He regarded his clipboard, looked up at her and said, "So I need to come in. To see it."

His voice filled with unmistakeable hesitation as his eyes dropped to below her chin, and tumbled down her front all the way to the floor. She crossed her arms across her middle to eliminate the feeling of being fully exposed, protecting herself from the sensation of him undressing her with his eyes. Heat gushed up her neck to her face as she thought of him imagining her body under the robe. Surely, she hadn't egged him on? How could she have when she didn't even know he was coming? "I will show you where it is. It's in the basement." The words no sooner escaped from her clumsy lips than she regretted saying them. Stupid sounding! Why couldn't she stop herself from saying things that red-flagged her awkwardness? "Well where else would it be?" she asked, as she led him downstairs, adding, "On the roof?" which made her sound even more daft. Why, oh why, didn't she shut her mouth, stop this silly exchange she was having with herself? She apologized for the mess in the basement, which wasn't that bad, really. Just a pile of things to be hauled off when she got around to it, but it was something to say.

She stood behind him and took in the breadth of his shoulders, his agility with his tools, despite the chubbiness of his fingers. Where the ribbing of the t-shirt ended at the fullest part of his biceps and grazed his skin, the most satisfying curve of muscle, a graceful arch, like something you might see in a painting in the hands of a master, the silken skin, the hint of a tan. However, she could not stand around here all day today watching him work, and it would be most unfortunate if he delayed her and caused lunch to be rushed. And no matter what, she had to get to the bank to transfer funds before the deadline date and her account rejected payments due to insufficient funds.

"Do you know how long this will take?" Her eyes still on the line where his t-shirt hugged his biceps.

He pushed back on his haunches, stared at the heater, seemed to speak to it. "Depends. On what I find. Sometimes we come across rust, even on a newer unit like this. You wouldn't think it. Or lime buildup on the elements. Keeps it from running at peak performance. Shows up in your monthly bill."

"It's just that I have to be somewhere."

"Shouldn't take long."

As if this loose approximation of time, after his unannounced intrusion into her morning, sufficed as an answer. She would take her leave from him. Now there was a curious turn of phrase. Good thing she didn't say it aloud. Where had it come from? She'd no idea where she'd picked that one up. She'd never read Jane Austen. Not that she could remember.

"I'm going upstairs. Call if you need me." Which, of course, was also ridiculous. She was going to help him, was she? Give him advice about the water heater?

On the way up the stairs, the phone rang. What now? Her hair to do, and time getting so limited after all the interruptions—though she didn't think of the oriole that way—she really should not have spent so long in the shower—she'd no time to iron anything to wear to lunch.

She grabbed the phone just before it went to answer, managed a breathless hello. On the other end, Lisa was practically shouting. Something about a squirrel and how it had to go to a vet because it wasn't quite dead and Bill couldn't bring himself to run over it with the car. It made a hideous screaming noise, kicked its legs like it was peddling a bike. In the gutter, twitching, and kicking and still alive, but too hurt to run away, and when Bill tried to pick it up, it snapped at him with its needle teeth. It would take two to take it to the vet. One to hold it, wearing protective gloves, the other to drive, because one bite from that squirrel could give one of them rabies, or diphtheria, or worse. Wendy doubted it, but didn't say so—hadn't those diseases been eliminated, or wherever they went? Once Lisa got notions in her head, she wasn't easily dissuaded. "I'll have to keep you posted. I am not sure what this will do to lunch. Maybe just delay it. I'll call when I know." Before she hung up, she was already shouting Bill's name.

On the way back to her bedroom, she glanced outside to the tree to see if the oriole was back. Not there. Not yet.

Wendy stood in front of the mirror, felt the slide of her housecoat along her arms, and confronted her naked body. She thought of the technician in the basement, his sausage-like chubby digits twitching at the end of his muscular arms, kneeling on her floor, fiddling with her plumbing. She thought of the taut pull of his t-shirt across the dense thickness of his arms. Her skin wasn't as wrinkly as it could be, and her muscles, though somewhat saggy, could have been a lot worse.

Look at her hair, way past the point where it could be styled easily, and not enough time to wet it again or put it in rollers, not with a man kneeling on her basement floor. She'd have to look a fright at lunch, well, half a fright, but what other way around it? And her outfit, now that she might have to run downstairs at a moment's notice, could not be the crisp blue blouse with the black slacks she'd planned, but the knit top, more of a tunic really, not very flattering, but it didn't need pressing, and her grey pants, a reliable standby. Not that Lisa would care or even notice, but it wasn't what she'd imagined wearing to the bank. No one would take you or your money seriously if you dressed haphazardly. They'd make assumptions, give you low-priority service. And look at the service she got yesterday—top-level. Elite, she'd call it. How else could she explain all the interest the teller showed in her? But it wasn't just that, was it? Let's be honest. She connected with him in a way that went beyond client courtesy. More of a friendship, if she had to label it, not fully formed—how could it be on such a short meeting?—but certainly evolving. *I look forward to seeing you again.*

What was that? Had she heard something? Muscle man in the basement, calling her? She tugged on the tunic and the pants and ran all the way down to the basement. He was still on his knees in front of the white tank, as if praying at an altar. "Do you need something?" she panted.

"Nope," he said. "So far, everything's checking out fine. How long did you say you had this?"

She didn't know. "Well, if you don't need me, I will run upstairs again."

"Yeah," he said. "Fine." He spoke as if he hadn't heard her, just said something, an automatic reply.

In her bedroom, Wendy leaned into the mirror. She turned her face this way and that to see if the light caught any of the fine white hairs that seemed to grow inches overnight and made her think of herself as some kind of root vegetable, something organic. She couldn't always catch them, then would find one, after a social event, and pluck it, an inch of embarrassment, and wonder who had seen it. She removed a few stray hairs out of her eyebrows and rubbed her face with lotion. Carefully, she took out the tools of her deceitfulness, the applicators that would erase years from her face: the foundation, the coverup, liner to create brows, mascara to imply lashes, and stepped back to look at her handiwork. Not bad. Presentable. For lunch and the gallery. Provided the day wasn't trashed by a half-dead squirrel. But definitely the bank. *Oh, it's so nice to see you again.* She could almost hear him.

A flicker of light had her turn to the doorway, and there stood the technician with his thick, inflated arms, his broad forehead square as a board. He looked superhuman, abnormal, monstrous. Now she knew he got in here under false pretenses, knew there was something about this that wasn't quite right or she would have received a notice from the property manager. "What are you doing here?" she said, tamping down her fear, pretending to stay cool and in control.

"I need you to sign this invoice," he thrust the paper out at her, but did not cross the threshold of her bedroom door. "I kept calling, but I don't think you heard me."

"I will come downstairs to sign that." With great emphasis she stated her terms, took control, as if she were Scarlett O'Hara resisting the takeover of Tara, insisting on a sense of decorum, using every ounce of caution she could find since a bed lurked just over there, piled high with luxurious, satin cushions. And still in her mind, his earlier stripping away of her robe with his eyes. Who knew what else he was thinking? Well, she could guess! "I'll be down forthwith. Shortly."

"Fine, but I need it fast. I've got a lot of stops today." His work boots thudded on the stairs.

When he'd gone, she made herself a cup of coffee and sat by the window, watching for the oriole, waiting for Lisa's call. Two o'clock and she still hadn't heard, held up by an impaired squirrel. It probably needed surgery and Lisa and Bill would be waiting for the results. They'd enough money to agree to surgery for the random rodent that sabotaged the day. Wendy would have taken it to the basement and put a hammer to its head. Or left it in the gutter and pretended it didn't exist. Eventually Lisa would call and say, *What else could we do? We couldn't just leave it. I wouldn't be able to sleep with it lying out there suffering.*

At three o'clock, she went upstairs to freshen her makeup. Since today's lunch was a bust, she'd go back to the bank and finish what she got too distracted to complete yesterday. One hour until the branch closed, and even if...*Noah!* That's right, that was his name! She knew it would come to her. Biblical sounding. Even if *Noah* had a huge line up, that should still give her enough time to wait in his line for a little conversation. Perhaps it was unusual for someone her age to form a friendship with someone so young, but who said there were rules to this? A couple of years shy of seventy, no one should think she had a foot in the grave.

Lucky day. There was Noah with only a few people in his line.

He looked up from his work a couple of times, didn't see her smile at him, so involved with his customers, giving terrific service, she could see. And didn't he look smart! Sharp as a tack!

The other people in the bank, waiting for the tellers, appeared so shabbily dressed she couldn't imagine they even had bank accounts, though that wasn't nice to think. But let's be honest; they'd gone to no effort to make themselves attractive. And especially for Noah in his fresh white shirt, open at the neck, and a black suit jacket, the white and black crisply contrasting, his hair slicked back off his forehead, his blue eyes beaming as he smiled through his work. A more handsome young man she'd rarely seen, and his hands, the way they danced over the keyboard bringing up accounts—the fingers of a pianist, smooth and silken.

Just one more person in front of her and she could hardly believe what Noah was saying to the woman who seemed, as far as Wendy could tell, to have saved up all her banking for today and was taking an exceptionally long time. "Have you any plans for tonight?" he asked. The exact same question he'd asked Wendy yesterday. But that was altogether different; he'd taken an interest in Wendy; they'd clicked. And obviously, he didn't have the same rapport with this woman. Look at her outfit. A mismatched sweatshirt, and sweatpants with pouchy knees. "I don't see how that is any business of yours what I'm doing tonight," the woman said, her voice surprisingly deep for someone who couldn't have weighed more than a hundred pounds.

Wendy gasped at her rudeness, her insolence, not quite believing what she'd heard, when all poor Noah was doing was trying to be nice. There was no chemistry between this woman and Noah, none at all. She wished she could relive their conversation yesterday, wished she had given him a more composed answer and remembered to do the rest of her banking, even after he specifically asked her if there was anything else he could do for her. After she told him she was going out for dinner that night with friends, named the restaurant, despite the terrible weather that flooded basements, but she'd heard good things about the restaurant, then they were going to a movie, one she'd read a review for that very morning in the paper, and he said he'd heard the movie was good. And he asked her if she'd seen another movie, one she'd never heard of, and she said not yet, and he said, "Make sure you do," and she said she certainly would, would make a note of it, though she couldn't even remember the name of it now. It didn't really matter—did it?—that she had no plans last night for dinner and a movie with friends, but she couldn't very well say nothing when he asked her, *Do you have any plans for tonight?*— she couldn't very well say, *I'm not doing anything. No plans.* Why not just come right out and say, I'm having a blah life, not very exciting?

And today, when he asked her what she was doing, because he was bound to, drawn in by her warmth and their mutual compatibility and the strong bond they'd established yesterday, she'd tell him about her dinner plans with a friend, a new friend, a technician. He didn't need to know that he fixed water heaters, or that he was much younger. She would see how the conversation went. He might be interested in the oriole, perhaps he liked birds, and if he did, it would be something else they had in common. She could bring her sightings diary to share with him the next time she came to him to do her banking.

The woman in the baggy sweats was taking forever to pack up her paper and envelopes and stuff them in an ancient purse that looked like she'd been sitting on it for twenty years. Wendy wanted to tell her to get on with it, didn't want to hear all her huffing and puffing—so oral, so graphic. Off-putting. As she continued to sort herself out, muttering all the time, Noah sat calmly before her, his long fingers laced together elegantly, then leaned closer and said very softly, as if he didn't want anyone else to hear, "Ma'am, we are encouraged to make communication contact points with our clients. It's corporate policy. To develop good customer relations and humanize the banking experience. Obviously, I don't really care what you're doing tonight."

Wendy gasped. He didn't mean it! He only said it because she was so rude to him, and Wendy didn't blame him, not one bit. She would have said worse to that nasty woman, put her in her place. *Get out of here and don't ever come back!* Wendy would reassure Noah when it was her turn. Don't let that woman affect our relationship, she would tell him. They'd so many topics to cover— books, birds, TV shows, restaurants, movies.

The woman gave Wendy a sour look as she stepped away from Noah's line and Wendy took her place in front of him. Wendy's eyes locked with Noah's and he asked, "How may I help you?" without so much as a glimmer of recognition or the slightest of smiles. But of course, he'd just had the stuffing taken out of him by Baggy Pants, and needed some recovery time. And her rude reaction would make him wary of everyone, even Wendy, his new friend. He needed to be handled tenderly, nurtured and eased into her transaction to reassure him he was safe with her. She wanted to reach across and cup his tender hands with hers, squeeze them. Before she could remind him she'd been in yesterday, which would encourage him back into their incredible bond and show he was no longer under the threat of any kind of verbal attack, he said, "That was unfortunate. I don't always agree with corporate policies to engage with clients. Doesn't always go over very well."

Wendy's hand trembled. She couldn't swipe her debit card to bring up her account. "I've forgotten something. Sorry. Sorry." She shoved the card in her pocket and stepped away.

"Ma'am. Ma'am," Noah called out. "You forgot your purse."

A corporate policy? That was what she was? Invited to spill her guts, tricked even, only to be forgotten? She'd made a fool of herself! She had to get out of here! The way he looked at her today, like just another customer. He had no memory of her from yesterday, no recollection of their conversation. The sharing of intimate details. How would she know ever again if someone was being real or not when they asked her a question? How would she know if anyone really cared?

She had to get home. To watch for the oriole, wait for that glorious dart of brightness that shot into her morning, a quick quiver of euphoria. What if it never came back? She'd never know unless she watched for it, an uncertainty she could rely on.

About the author:

Catharine Leggett's short stories have appeared in the anthologies *The Empty Nest* (KY Story), *Law & Disorder* (Main Street Rag), *Best New Writing 2014* (Hopewell), as well as in the journals *Room*, *Event*, *The New Quarterly*, *Canadian Author*, and *The Antigonish Review*. Other stories have appeared online in *paperbytes*, *Per Contra*, *Margin: Exploring Modern Magical Realism* (novel excerpt), and broadcast on CBC Radio. A novel, *The Way to Go Home* (Urban Farmhouse Press), will appear early in 2019. A collection of short stories, *In Progress*, won the Eludia Award and will be published by Sowilo Press (imprint of Hidden River Publishing) in 2019. This is her fifth story to be published by Scribes Valley. She lives in London, Ontario, Canada.

WOOD AVENUE
©2019 by Virginia M. Amis

Mt. Rainier, barometer of weather and daily cheerfulness to those relying on its forecast, gave a half-hearted appearance on this Northwest fall morning. Make up your mind, I admonished, watching as its top disappeared from view, but its shoulders remained steadfast against the cloud cover. I smiled at its stubbornness, moved by its singular beauty. Above it, red streaked against the early horizon, teasing, but never producing its source. Judging from the lackluster participation, I divined that our mountain would remain halfway hidden for a while, not sure whether to bring luck to bear on the day or to leave us wondering.

My driver, who wore a band matching mine, grumbled at the SUV that cut him off as the road narrowed from three lanes to two. I didn't understand his upset. We nearly always left home in plenty of time to reach our destination before the opening hymn. Sometimes, we arrived so early the lights were not yet raised to full brightness and the seniors, who spoke to each other too loudly in the atrium, looked at us as though we'd come without an invitation.

I rode along in silence, content to watch the day from my seat with no responsibility other than to not be contrary. Experience had told me my comments on the SUV situation might not be appreciated. It also told me if I were to direct his attention away from the road, toward the mountain, the resulting "uh-huh" would be less than satisfying.

The view across the harvested valley moved me to awe. I wanted to stop, drink in its sweetness and feel smug that I had been granted an audience. How many people had been invited? How many declined? How many more skies would appear in such splendor?

I knew mine was a child's reaction. So what? Though childhood had bid goodbye decades ago, I felt entitled to draw upon its privileges, since they had been denied when my hair hung in braids down my back. Too busy with helping raise my siblings to remember to roll my body down a grassy knoll, laugh raucously at silly jokes or stare at cloud art, my youth had passed quickly into adulthood before I noticed what I had missed. Opportunities to languish on lazy summer days, when lightning bugs landed on soft arms, to build mud pies and swing carelessly on playground sets, were gone by the time I realized I'd never taken my turn. Saddened, I contented myself to read about them in stories.

But, if I thought these thrills were not to be, I'd been mistaken. Joy was not a mean provider. Who can say when it's too late to feel a simple thrill? Thirty, forty, seventy or eighty? Delayed did not mean denied. Joy persisted at my door, pricked my skin and surged unexpectedly through my bloodstream. She nudged, suggested, winked, laughed. Saved up and overflowing, she demanded I notice her. I wanted to pay her homage.

My husband hit the brakes, mumbling something uncharitable toward another driver. He gave me a sorry smile and glared ahead.

Returning my gaze to the mountain, I didn't plan to swing or roll down a hill, but to note joy's presence in other ways. I'd been given sunrises and mountains to appreciate. I had laughing skies and sharp hickory fires on cold days. Soft cotton sheets and woolen blankets comforted me during long, dark nights. Vegetable soup and peach pies warmed me from within. Life sparkled now and then and, bursting childlike, I'd let joy have her way with me.

We approached the traffic light at Wood Avenue. My driver cursed as he stopped the car on red, seeing no other vehicles.

"Why do we always have to stop here? Why can't this light be more responsive when no other traffic is around?" he asked, his knuckles white on the steering wheel.

Lovingly, I didn't answer. Instead, I stared at the golden-leafed maple that had been switched on to full color sometime in the last week. Set against the red-streaked sky with a clouded mountain backdrop, I said a silent "thank you."

I longed to share my joy with him. Maybe when the leaves fell, and were scooped and readied for compost, I will grab his hand and pull him into the raked pile, squealing with delight.

About the author:

Virginia Amis is a lawyer and a writer, who spends her days in the courtroom and her nights and weekends writing. A transplant from Pittsburgh to the Pacific Northwest, she writes in that setting, bringing nature and characters to life through her stories. She has written two fiction novels and is working on a third. Her short stories have been published in *Perspectives Magazine* and *101words.com*. An avid reader, she will devour most any novel in record time.

THE WHISPERERS
©2019 by Patricia L. Baker

I can hear them now...whispering. With their majestic, human-like forms, saguaro cacti have been guarding the canyon pass for thousands of years, passing judgment on all who dare to enter. Now, after all these years, I hear them. They are whispering to me. I know what they want. So, I sit here and watch and wait...thinking about how this all began.

Everyone told me I was crazy to marry Sam, and even crazier to move to Arizona, but I detested my life in the East and wanted desperately to leave the crowds and anonymity of the city. Most of all, I wanted space between my family and me. They were suffocating me, controlling my life and pushing me into a career I was beginning to despise. Then Sam came along. We met by accident when we literally bumped into each other on the street. The force of that bump knocked the books from my arms and my heart into his hands. As Sam retrieved each book and handed it to me, he read out loud each title and commented on each story. As he handed the last book to me, he suggested we go for coffee. I agreed, and it was at that moment I knew I was in love with this dark-eyed stranger.

When I took Sam to meet my family, they tried everything to dissuade me from going out with him. When he returned to Arizona, they were so relieved. But I cried for days afterwards. I wrote to him every day, pouring my heart out. He in turn described the land of his ancestors. His letters just affirmed for me how bleak my life was. When he eventually proposed, I immediately accepted. We were married in the small desert town where he was raised. From that point on I never heard from my parents even though I tried to keep in contact.

When I first saw the house in the canyon, I knew I made the right decision to marry Sam. The house was nestled in a slight valley, surrounded by saguaros and mountains. Although Sam's letters painted such beautiful pictures of the desert landscape, I was unprepared for the actual lushness of the desert and the human-like qualities of the saguaros. As Sam drove me through the canyon that first time, I saw these enormous green columns rising out of the rocky terrain. Unruly white flowers encircled their heads, while their arms were raised as if waving to me. They appeared playful and welcoming, beckoning me to enter the canyon. And, when I did, I felt as if the saguaros were observing me. When I asked Sam about this, he explained the legend of the saguaros.

Long ago, the saguaros were great human warriors who roamed the land. Eventually the warriors began to die off, but no one really knows why. As each warrior fell to the ground and died, a small seedling took the dead warrior's place. Over time, these seedlings grew into giant saguaros. But the saguaros remembered when they had human souls and bodies, and not those awkward arms and thorned ribs. So, at night they whispered among themselves and devised a plan to steal the human souls and bodies of the dying. Thus, the saguaros would become great human warriors once again.

Sam added that when the desert night is at its most quiet and if you listen very closely, you can hear the saguaros whispering. His story made me shiver, but I was so excited about seeing Sam's house that I forgot what he told me.

Sam built his house with the help of his brothers, and over time we added to its rough-hewn beauty. Sam loved the land with a passion and would tell me his ranch was the biggest accomplishment of his life second to marrying me. I always laughed over that comment, but I swear he knew every saguaro that guarded the canyon pass, and if nature made changes in the landscape, Sam was the first to notice. During the winter, when temperatures dropped thirty degrees, we spent many an hour just reading to each other or just loving each other. It was a wonderful existence, and our youth and joy of learning about each other and the surrounding land, drew us as close to each other as the saguaros that guarded the canyon. As much as Sam and I loved each other, children never happened. We accepted our barrenness because the land produced more than we could.

We were getting older and the sun weathered us to fine leathery specimens. When I looked in the mirror, I no longer saw that carefree, contented girl, but saw instead a watchful and waiting woman. In my eyes, Sam was still as handsome as when I first met him, but his once black hair was a soft gray. We had all that we'd ever wanted, and I wanted it to last forever.

Sam, however, was growing restless. At odd times I would find him among the saguaros, looking up at some of them, and nodding, as if in agreement. Then it began at night, the sounds like whispering. In the morning, I swore some of the saguaros moved during the night, so slightly and closer to the house. When I mentioned this to Sam, he disagreed, but smiled.

Time has a way of moving forward whether one wants it or not. Sam's entire family was gone. It was just the two of us in the canyon. Each day as we walked or sat outside, it seemed as if the saguaros were watching us and patiently waiting. But what were they watching and waiting for?

Sam was surprised when I first mentioned I wanted to leave our home. I told him, we were too old to stay by ourselves in such an isolated area. Sam's hair was pure white and his back was slightly bent. It took him a long time to finish any chore and many times I had to remind him what he was doing. I was tired in both mind and spirit and when I looked in the mirror, I didn't recognize the person looking back. My hair was as white as Sam's. Although the years of hard work kept me slim, my face was as wrinkled as the dried, hard ground. My hands were gnarled and displayed a river of blue veins.

Sam didn't want to leave the canyon. He was born here and he was going to die here. But I wasn't. I didn't want to stay any longer, because not only was he beginning to frighten me, so were the saguaros. They appeared to be different, maybe even more human-like.

Each night Sam would get up and pace. The pacing would only stop when he went outside and sat among the saguaros. There in the night, whether it was the merciless heat of summer or the cold wind of winter, he would find peace. I would observe Sam at these times, and when I did, I could see the slight swaying of the saguaros and hear their whispering.

I was determined to leave the canyon now, but wouldn't leave Sam. He needed me and I still loved him with all of my heart, but the constant whispering was becoming intolerable. It gnawed at me, eating into my soul. Yet, Sam didn't seem to be bothered by it. I was beginning to think the whispering was maybe a figment of my imagination.

That fateful night, the sky was velvety black and star studded. It was easy to pick out the constellations; something Sam and I always enjoyed doing. But that night Sam was in bed just as the sun set. I thought it odd and noted he looked even more worn and tired than usual. No sooner did his eyes close than the whispering began. It would ebb and flow. Louder and softer. Few voices and then many. I frantically covered my ears to block out the sounds, but nothing could block the sounds of the Whisperers.

As I watched over Sam that night, his breathing was shallow and the rattle of death rose above the Whisperers' voices. Fear was creeping into my very being because I knew the Whisperers were coming for Sam. The legend wasn't a legend at all.

No amount of pleading to the gods could change what was happening. When I looked closer, I saw the Whisperers swaying ever so slightly, moving closer and closer to the house, whispering Sam's name. Beckoning.

Sam stirred slightly and finally settled into the sleep of no return. As I sat vigil over Sam, I dozed. When I woke, Sam was gone. No physical evidence of him remained. He was now one with the Whisperers. And I was alone.

I mourned for him as a lost soul howling at the wind. I thought of suicide, but it wasn't in my nature. Somehow time passed. I decided to leave the canyon, as there was nothing or no one to hold me back. I began packing, knowing I would be leaving a lifetime behind. I thought I was empty of tears, but I still cried. Weary from packing, I sat in Sam's chair and felt his warmth all around me.

That's when it began, ever so lightly, the whispering. I thought it was my imagination, but I know in my heart they are whispering my name. A gentle breeze touches my cheek, and I hear it as plain as day. They are calling to me. The Whisperers are back. Their sound is so inviting, so soothing.

I doze and dream of Sam. When I wake, the night sky holds a thousand stars. I can see the outlines of the Whisperers. I can see them moving closer and closer, murmuring, crooning, and purring ever so softly my name. The Whisperers are here. All I can do is sit and wait.

Until I am one with the Whisperers.

About the author:
Patricia L. Baker, currently a resident of Maryland, lived for 13 years in Arizona and before Arizona lived in New York for over 30 years. Prior to her move to Maryland, most of her writing was academic in nature with a few fictional pieces sprinkled in. It is her fascination with the saguaro cactus and Sabino Canyon, which she considers to be one of the most beautifully serene places to visit, inspired her to write "The Whisperers."

PICTURES AND STORIES AND GHOSTS
©2019 by Michelle Wotowiec

There are boxes on top of boxes filled with pictures covering the living room coffee table. On the couch sits Great Aunt Jane, my grandmother's older sister. She wears her cotton floral muumuu and salmon colored slippers that are so old her big toes have broken through the fabric. Her skin is the color of a fresh peach with bruises on the cheeks. Melanomas, she says.

Great Aunt Jane's been lonely, I know, and I remind myself this as I get comfortable on the couch next to her. She is proud and doesn't tell me she is lonely, but I see it. I see her loneliness in her countless phone calls to her children and grandchildren. Phone calls about whether or not they have caller ID and does the caller ID ever not work for them? She has been having some trouble with hers. About whether or not they heard there was a storm coming (she has some extra umbrellas if anyone wants to stop by and borrow one). And about if they were planning to use her Fry's VIP card this month for the gasoline discount—the discount will expire in the next couple weeks.

I see her loneliness on Saturdays and Sundays when she wishes me good morning in song before she takes her 6:00 am cup of coffee. I see it on Saturdays and Sundays as she rummages through her closet looking for just the right outfit—when she asks me whether a blue blouse and blue capris is too much blue. I see it after she is all dressed, her hair and make-up done, and she sits on her couch to watch *Judge Judy* or *People's Court*. After a while, she gets bored of court TV and shuffles over to her computer desk to check her Facebook page or play a couple of rounds of *Words with Friends*. Then she goes back to her couch. Then she is back to her computer desk, checking the answering machine every hour or so, until about 6:00 pm when she changes back into her muumuu. And then repeat. And repeat.

My grandmother, Aunt Jane's sister, wasn't sure what to say to me after the miscarriage. She knew I was broken—broken in a way I had never been before—and I think she thought me spending time with Aunt Jane would make me feel better.

Aunt Jane was born in 1938. The idea of eighty years passing takes my mind away from loneliness and into the concept of time. Imagining how much has changed in eighty years. How each second added into another and found a minute and the minutes found hours and the hours found days and the days found weeks and the weeks found months and the months found years and the next thing we know, we have gone from 1938 to 2018. I tell her about this thought as we sit together on her couch sipping Sangrias. She laughs and tells me that I really have no idea. She says time is so much more than minutes and seconds and days and months and that time is life—it's her life.

"It's these pictures," she says and pulls out an old faded photograph of her in a pinstriped dress, seven years old, standing next to her two younger cousins who were dressed in matching onesies, blonde hair combed to the side, smiles on their faces—real smiles, not the practiced-picture-smiles. "This is Charlie, my first cousin on my father's side," she says, pointing to the boy on the right. I take a closer look and notice he has a deep dimple in his left cheek. "I remember exactly when this picture was taken. Isn't that funny?" She says, "That I can go back to that exact moment in my memory when there are so many other, more important things I just can't recall?"

I nod and hand the picture back to her.

"Anyway, we were back at Aunt Gennie's in Elyria. She had a nice little house that had a backyard that went right up to the river. It was a warm day for being in September. I asked Charlie that day what he wanted for Christmas, and you know what he said?" She pauses and waits for me to guess.

"I don't know, what?" I ask.

"He said," she stops to let out a small cough. Aunt Jane started smoking at thirteen years old and only recently kicked the habit—recently enough that the house still smells stale. If I breathe too deeply, I can still get the taste of smoke on my tongue. She clears her throat, and continues, "He said he wanted a *toot toot* train." She laughs and her top lip curls above her bottom. The wrinkles lining her eyes remind me of my grandmother, her sister, back in Cleveland. Grandma Trudy is younger than Aunt Jane, but they've reached the age where a few years really means nothing more than a few extra stories to tell. And these ladies sure are story tellers. "It was a shame, what happened to those boys," Aunt Jane says with a tang of melancholy that engulfs the room.

My husband complains that Aunt Jane is a talker—she talks and talks and never gives anyone a chance to chime in. She doesn't even expect a response, he says, simply a nod. He is tired of nodding—he just isn't good at it—and would rather be in the office on his computer doing research. He has never been much of a people person. I tell him that she has eighty years of stories and we owe it to her to listen to them. We should want to listen to them.

She tells me that Charlie's father was a drunk—a drunk veteran—and he was supposed to be watching six-year-old Charlie and his four-year-old brother Andrew. Andrew liked to go by Andy and how he sure did have a smile—a smile that could just melt your heart. You would think two boys that age wouldn't get along, she said, but those boys were like two peas in a pod. Always sharing their toys and Charlie knew it was his job to take care of little Andy—that is what a big brother does, he once told Aunt Jane and she just thought it was the cutest thing.

The boys' mother, Gennie, was off getting some milk and eggs that cold January morning. They didn't have a car back then, Aunt Jane says; a lot of people didn't. "So, Gennie had to go on foot," she continues. "She told her husband to watch those boys, but when she got back from the store, he was out cold on the living room floor and the boys were nowhere to be found."

This story is about to take a bad turn, I can tell, as tears form in her eyes, and makes me think that maybe my husband is right. Maybe I should head out. Save myself from the words that will undoubtedly linger. But, instead, I listen.

Well, they were found early the following morning, Charlie with his head below the frozen water, blue and bloated, icy and cold, and Andy about a half a mile down at the bottom of the river. The coyotes had taken some of him, but he was still identifiable. Once she put the story into the space between us, it was there for good. I couldn't erase it and she couldn't take it back. In a way, she breathed a quick breath into Charlie's bloated body seventy years later. A breath I inhaled and swallowed and would fight in my dreams for days to come. Weeks to come. Who knows how long to come?

My husband and I had been staying with her for the past two months. Sitting on the couch, I start to tally up the stories I have collected and retained in the past eight weeks:

1. Aunt Jane was knocked up at seventeen. She says it all happened very fast. Tom courted her when she was fourteen. He was eighteen and she was fourteen and he was so handsome with his hair parted to the left. He had deep brown eyes and a shadow of a beard. He told her she was the most beautiful thing he had ever laid his eyes on and begged her to wait for him. He was being deployed to a war he had to fight and he begged her to wait for him. Three years later, barely able to contain themselves, it happened. She said she knew better but it was love and love makes you do dumb shit.

2. Shortly before the wedding, Tom, the father of the baby growing inside her belly and the man who told her she

was the most beautiful thing he had ever laid eyes on only three short years earlier, was supposed to pick her up after her night class (she was kicked out of high school once she began to show and had to complete her final credits at night classes) to take her on a dinner date. Just a cheap, easy-going dinner, she said. But a date nonetheless. She was having a hard time, she said, and he wanted to make her feel loved. Show her that she was still the apple of his eye, even though she had gained forty pounds and looked like a beachball. Instead of picking her up after class, though, he went out to the bar down on Detroit and 57th Street with some friends. He forgot about her, and as she stood there outside a dark parking lot waiting, she told herself she would never marry the fucker.

3. Well, they did marry and she says she regrets it to this day. Six grown children and sixty-three years later, she says she knew pretty quickly that it wasn't supposed to be. Fate? I asked her. No, not fate, she said. Common fucking sense. The guy was a drunken asshole.

4. Tom was Catholic and didn't believe in birth control, although now she says she doesn't understand how she agreed to not believe in something so important, and the babies just kept coming. The next thing she knew she was pregnant again. And again. And again. And again, until she had six children, all a year apart. Well, that isn't entirely true. There was a miscarriage in-between—one she said that was left in the toilet on a Friday night and the doctor wasn't available to tell her what to do with it until Monday.

5. She lost a child. A grown child, but her child nonetheless. She says that you never really understand what it's like

to lose a child until you lose one. Sure, you can close your eyes and imagine the idea of someone being there one day and gone the next. You can imagine their chair at the dinner table being empty. You can imagine the phone never ringing. You can imagine all sorts of things, but it isn't the same and you really have no idea what it is like until it happens. It is crying at random smells that remind you of his face. And then his face—it runs through your memory like a slideshow—birth to the first birthday party, to the first day of kindergarten, and so on. It is making dinner one minute and feeling a hole inside you the next, a hole so big it knocks the wind out of you. It's realizing that hole is him—he has become a hole inside your chest.

I have some stories to tell too. I could describe the moments of anticipation after peeing on a pregnancy test. I could describe how those moments, after two years of trying with no luck, started to define my very being. I could tell her how every moment became heavy. How much I began to hate my own body for not being able to do the one thing it was truly meant to do. I didn't have a photograph to attach this story to, though, so I didn't bother going into it.

Aunt Jane and I are going through these pictures together for her birthday party. One of her sons wants to put together a collage to display in his living room. This is going to be the biggest event in her life in quite some time—all five living children and their grandchildren and their children will be there. She doesn't remember the last time they have all been together. She skips through any of the pictures that make her look fat—she says she had some weight issues at times and would rather not see those pictures at her birthday party. She laughs at this, so I laugh too.

I look back down at the black and white picture she pulled out of the box—she was young, twenty, with her daughter Dorothy, six months old, on her lap, her husband (before he was a drunk but after he returned from the war), with her son Tommy Jr, two years old, on his lap. In the picture, Aunt Jane had her brown curly hair cut into a short bob and she wore pearl earrings. Her smile looked real, showing her straight white teeth and red lips. She says now that the smile was real, sort of. She says she knew she was in for the long haul, and there was something, dammit to hell, about Tom that she really did love, but she also knew, somewhere inside her, that it wasn't the path she wanted.

Nicky, child #4, would die in his forties. He had a drinking problem and an anger problem (like his father) and one night he was found dead in the backyard. His skin was changing colors. The conversation goes to him sometimes, and I can always tell when it does because her voice cracks and tears slip their way down her cheeks. She says that it's easy to judge him and say he was a loser. Two divorces, spent some time in jail, drank a lot. That's what everyone saw, she says, and that's what killed him. He learned to see himself the way others saw him. She says no one else saw the little surprises he would leave around her house when he would come to visit. They didn't see the little *Star Wars* trinkets he would hide in her bathroom vanity for her to find after he left. Or the voicemails he would leave for her, just short, quick *I love you, Mom* messages she would come home to every so often. She pulls out his baby pictures to show me his face before it became what I saw in the pictures of his later life.

She shows me a black and white photo of her during her third pregnancy. She still has the same beehive hairdo but has stopped wearing so much make-up. She runs her finger across her belly in the photograph and tells me that being a mother is what she was meant to be. That in all these years, the thing that matters most, is being a mother. She won't be around forever, she says, but in a way, she will live on. Gennie, Charlie and Andy's mother knew it. That's why she was never the same once she was no longer a mother. Light tears dampen her cheeks and she doesn't care to wipe them dry. She's earned them, I imagine she feels at this very moment.

This new moment, in 2018, sitting on her couch digging through boxes of pictures she hasn't looked at in years, is ours to share. I don't want to tell her the story about my husband and I trying to get pregnant for the past two years. I don't want to go into detail about the planning, and the names we originally chose, how those names have transformed into elephants—into tiny bombs that could set me on fire. How the idea of being a mother had overcome me—it had become every part of my being and it was killing me knowing it was out of reach. I could tell her about the afternoon when my husband told me that our story will be just fine if it ends up being the two of us. We would still be happy. I could describe to her how that one moment in time was frozen and saved to replay over and over and over again—how it was my life raft. I could tell her how I was luckier than her, well lucky enough to find myself a good one—a real good one. Instead though, I listen.

After hours of going through old pictures pass, I wash our Sangria glasses and kiss my husband goodnight. I do not know, then, that Aunt Jane's COPD would get the best of her in just three short months—that her last coherent words to me would be "How is the baby?" and I wouldn't have the heart to tell her I had lost it—that my body had once again decided against becoming a mother. I would nod and hold my breath in deep as tears slid down my cheeks.

I don't know any of this as I fall into a dream of an ocean that night. There is no land in sight—just endless dark blue-black water in every direction. I am in a kayak with no paddles with Great Aunt Jane. There are no husbands or children, just the two of us. I realize that she is crying and I feel my entire body freeze—I do not know what to do or what to say. But wait- that's wrong. At closer look, she is laughing. Actually, *we* are laughing. She tells me that she has been talking to Nicky and could I believe it? He is doing so well for himself. She tells me that her life may be coming to an end sooner, rather than later, but it has been one hell of a life and she is happy to have lived it. She tells me that after second thought, maybe there is more to life than being a mother. Anyone can be a mother, you know? It is about being a teacher—being good. Being someone who is inherently good—someone who, at the end of it all, will know who they were, what they come from, and be proud of who they have become. That's how goodness spreads, right?

I nod. We both become silent as we realize we have no paddles—no way of finding shore. "What will we do?" I ask her.

"We jump in," she says.

The next morning, I tell my husband (who doesn't drink Sangrias) that we should listen to her stories together. There is something important here and it is within our reach. We should sit on that couch, take up space, and let her talk. Soak it all in. Let her get those stories through her lips and breathe in those people of her past. This is what it is all about. Pictures and stories and ghosts.

About the author:

Michelle was born and raised in Spencer, Ohio, (population 800!). She would realize only in adulthood just how unique such an upbringing would be. Through college, she spent her free time bartending and waiting tables. After completing her graduate degree at Cleveland State University, Michelle relocated to Phoenix to teach college-level English and literature courses.

Her realistic fiction is inspired by her diverse experiences and the spirited people she has encountered along the way. She takes pride in being introspective and looking for the common humanity we all share, regardless of where we come from – the little things that connect us and have the power to inspire kindness and understanding.

"Pictures and Stories and Ghosts" is an ode to her late great aunt and the time spent while living with her for four months in 2017. She hopes the words do her unique and spunky aunt's epic storytelling justice and act as a way to keep her alive—breathing—in a way that only stories can.

Michelle is honored to once again be published by Scribes Valley Publishing. Michelle would like to thank her husband for his love and support.

SELTZER CAN ON A BLUE TRACTOR PAINTED ORANGE

©2019 by Steve Putnam

Sitting on the back deck of our house in a woodland gone house lot, we're looking outward, at an old Ford tractor sitting at the wood's edge, a seltzer can on its exhaust stack, log winch hitched to the rear. Under the darkening horizon of a downswing sun, I'm treating restless fatigue with a shot, a beer, and another beer. Crickets—I can't tell—fifty, fifty thousand vibrating like fiddles warped out of tune. Disharmony's strangely peaceful. I'm tired of putting down hardwood. Cut, fit, nail; cut, fit, nail. Knees, fingers, wrists in pain, hard to imagine old-time carpenters with nothing but hammers and hand saws getting the same job done.

Hardwood factory-finished, oak stained and coated shiny rustic dark or light; lumbered wood meets standards of perfection. Living room and hall connected, messes my mind with a mental fog you get trying to untangle geometry that pits perfection against reality. Compare measurements from three different points. Determine first row placement, so the floor runs in near perfect parallel with the opposite wall where it ends.

Air nail gun echoes like a .22 caliber on steroids. Ear muff protection makes the head sweat, converts harsh bangs into pleasant thumps. Chop saw's high frequency crosscut grind, portable table saw's threatening rip. Measure, stand, kneel, cut, go back, kneel, fit; stand up, swing the hammer, trigger the nail gun. So, the hardwood goes, two and a quarter inches wide at a time.

Dee's father G's house, an American dream driven by back-tax reality, ninety-acre woodlot sold for development supported his retirement. Developer dropped G's old house, ran a new road, planted new houses. Part of the deal, he relocated G.'s tractor and logging winch out back behind this new ranch at the barren backyard's edge under trees.

Time to install hardwood, no time for the garden. Fruits of neglect, weeds as high as a pint-size elephant's eye, huge pepper plants barren, tomatoes draught-starved, stunted but ripe.

Framed by borderline trees, Ford 3000 tractor stares back at us. Whole thing's painted ugly orange instead of Ford tractor blue. Sheet metal over the engine's decaled, "Allis Chalmers." Beer keg size, propane tank painted silver, mounted on the front left. Rear tires down four or five inches in pine needles and dirt, sinking back into the earth, bit by bit over the last twenty years, hinting a new world nightmare.

Dee's late husband arranged the deal, got the tractor cheap from a food warehouse. She can't give it up. "Keep it in the family," she says. "Send it out to Jr."

"He's halfway across the country. Cost more to ship than it's worth."

"It was my father's."

"Can't hang a tractor on the wall like a knick knack. It's not exactly a plaque or trophy. Blue painted orange makes it an ugly lawn ornament"

I remember G. removing the muffler, covering the exhaust stack with a shiny, silver yellow aluminum seltzer can, delaying the tractor's self-destruction, buying time, keeping rain water and summer humidity from wandering down the exhaust manifold, past a valve or two, into the cylinders. I remember him jacking the front axle with an old-fashioned screw jack, taking weight off the tires so they'd last, saving them for next time he'd need to pull out more firewood, maybe clear an estate lot, build a cabin with a wood stove, a garden outside

G got old, sold logs directly to a guy who pulled them out of the woods with a big-assed skidder, not a wimpy tractor winch. Trucked them out on a flat-bed rig, who knows where they ended up?

Maybe the back-lot hardwood floated to China, through finishing vats, back to the U.S.A., to be sold by Liquid Lumbernators, discounters of American Dreams. By chance, does the shiny hardwood floor come from the same trees that stood here? As far as I know, American hardwood gets barged over to China these days, returns factory finished.

So here I am, putting in a hardwood floor, thinking about G trucking his own logs to the mill, picking out the widest board for a bar top. Here I am, selling a mongrel warehouse tractor with a logging winch, converted from propane to gas, stranded on an island, surrounded by McMansions sporting hardwood floors.

Years of sitting in one place, moisture made its way into the tractor's cylinders. Pistons bound by rusted cylinder walls; the engine's frozen. Three times, I pulled the spark plugs, poured in Marvel Mystery Oil hoping it would free the rust.

Farmer who owns fifty cows that produce organic milk, drives more than a hundred miles to check out the tractor. Not prone to small talk, he spends every ounce of energy wisely, wasting no words. "What's an old tractor doing in a place like this?" he asks. Orange Ford tractor decaled Allis Chalmers, surrounded by McMansions, lawns you could almost golf on while your eggs fry on near-perfect asphalt pavement, makes his question a good one.

Farmer checks the dipstick for antifreeze in the oil, checks the radiator for oil in the antifreeze, tries turning the fan, confirming the engine's frozen. He walks around, inspecting the tires. "I don't know," he says, "I can get the hydraulics for three hundred, shipped to my door. If I buy this, I don't know what I'm getting. It'll cost five hundred more just for transport. Seven fifty's the best you can do?"

Over the phone, I've already dropped the price from nine to seven fifty. Instead of making a counter offer say, "I understand."

"I don't want to insult," he says. "Throw in that winch. I'll take a chance at eight hundred. My brother will kill me if he finds how much I paid."

Farmer turns his back, steps into the woods, out of sight of neighbors. Back turned, he takes a leak. Now that his brother's part of the negotiation, I get on my cell, call Dee, who's in the house close by. It is her tractor, so I explain. "Guy's a straight shooter, he needs the hydraulics. Right place, right time, it might be worth more."

"You're throwing in the winch and you're down to eight hundred? Sleep on it," she says.

Week later, farmer hands me eight crisp hundred-dollar bills, loads the tractor on the trailer. Front right tire flat, it sits lopsided. Without ceremony, he pulls the seltzer can from the exhaust, most likely to keep it from bouncing off onto the road. He hands it to me.

Another down swing sun, moonlight framed in broken clouds turns darkness peaceful. Crickets fiddle the same out of tune tunes. We're sitting out on the deck, staring out at the void at the wood's edge where the tractor sat for years. Donor parts keep another Ford 3000 running, help a farm survive, or at least prolong the agony. No more hardwood floor until tomorrow. I'm having another shot and beer. Seltzer can only worth a nickel in a bottle redemption machine, worth more balanced on the deck rail, a memorial to a tractor I can't call ugly, a nod to G.

About the author:

Steve Putnam lives in Western Massachusetts, in ancestral shadows of farmers, carpenters, and ice dealers. He has worked as a laborer, G.M. mechanic, framing carpenter. Last gig as a copier tech, he worked in schools, prisons, hospitals, and a scrap yard or two. Putnam also guest starred as copier repairman under the corporate florescence of a large life insurance company. He often paddles marathon canoes, solo or tandem with wife, Cynthia.

His novel, *Academy of Reality* and novel in progress excerpt, "School of Agriculture," both made the finalist list in the 2018

Faulkner-Wisdom Competition in New Orleans. His short fiction pieces have appeared in *Whiskey Island Magazine, Carbon Culture Review* online, and his non-fiction book, *Nature's Ritalin for the Marathon Mind*, was published by Upper Access.

THE MALLEABILITY OF MEMORY

©2019 by Ronna L. Edelstein

Ronna L. Edelstein dedicates "The Malleability of Memory" to her mother, Anne Edelstein, a woman who tried her best, which is all anyone can do.

"Bubbaleh, your mother and I want you to join us in Florida for some rest and relaxation."

Even through the phone, Vera hears Dad smiling—and lying. Of course, he wants Vera to fly to Florida for the long Thanksgiving weekend because he and Vera are more than father and daughter; they are best friends. He also understands that the first Thanksgiving without her pre-teen son and daughter—the newly signed divorce decree states that the kids spend this holiday with their father—will be tough for Vera.

But Vera also knows that the "Ma wants you to join us" part is a benign lie created by Dad. Ever since Ma had started working at a neighborhood children's store when Vera had turned twelve, she has lived an even more regimented life that excludes quality time with Vera. "You allow your son too much freedom," she always criticizes. "Why don't you ever clean your daughter's room? I used to go into your room all the time to throw out things I didn't think you needed," she boasts. And the worst dig of all: "You look like you're gaining weight," she tsk-tsks as she pinches the roll of skin above the elastic waistband of Vera's pants. Yes, Dad is turning reality into fiction—he knows, and he knows that Vera knows that Ma is not eager to share her first holiday in decades with Vera, the daughter who is just never enough to satisfy Ma. Vera can only imagine the emotional arm twisting that has resulted in Ma's agreeing to Vera's visit.

"The hotel assured us that there is a small suite available due to a last-minute cancellation," Dad explains. "You will have your own room, but we will all share the same bathroom, just like we did when you were a little girl."

Vera hopes the bathroom comes with a lock. As a child, she would be performing her ablutions when Ma, without announcing her intentions, would enter the bathroom. The noun "privacy" does not exist in Ma's personal lexicon—unless it is *her* privacy under consideration.

No, Ma will not enjoy Vera's company at the beach, but Vera— after dealing with many frazzled hours with her two children, still discombobulated from the pre-divorce tension and the finality of the divorce, and too many days of skidding and sliding over icy roads to and from work—convinces herself that she deserves a break, even under Ma's watchful eye. After a few minutes of contemplation, then, she chooses to accept Dad's invitation as a release, albeit a temporary one, from the turbulence of her life as a single mother, middle school teacher, and unhappy woman. She deludes herself into believing that a few days with Ma, with Dad as mediator and buffer, cannot be as bad as spending the holiday home alone.

Vera's arrival reinforces her certainty that she has made the correct decision. The sun sits in the sky—a large golden dinner plate against a freshly laundered blue tablecloth. It smiles upon the palm trees that, standing in even rows, separate the beach from the luxuriant hotels. The rays of the sun warm the chilly morning waters of the ocean, protecting the few early bird swimmers from the frigid sting of the salt. As she heads to the line of taxis, Vera feels her muscles loosening and her headache subsiding. Only when Vera arrives at the hotel and sees Dad and

Ma waiting for her in the lobby does she remember that Ma is a part of her retreat. Although Ma looks lovely, already tan after only a few days of basking in the sun, Vera knows Ma is a red rose—beautiful to look at but full of thorns that draw blood without warning; for Ma, Vera will always be a dandelion, a source of disappointment.

As Vera hugs and kisses Dad and pecks Ma on the cheek, she wonders if it is possible that she and Ma can have a good time together.

Vera passes the first day in the vacation paradise busying herself with the hustle and bustle of unpacking, discovering the ins-and-outs of the hotel, and refusing to take off her beach robe so that Ma cannot comment on the imperfections her bathing suit reveals. Once settled, she spends time gathering shells on the shore with Dad, leaving Ma, a skeleton oozing with baby oil, lounging near the pool to further bake herself in the sun. Vera tries to convince herself that this together-but-separate arrangement might work.

Even Thanksgiving dinner is tolerable. The hotel maître d' seats Vera and her parents at a large table with other guests. These guests become human barriers that protect Vera from Ma's acerbic comments about the number of bites of stuffing she has taken, about her saying "yes" to having ice cream added to her pumpkin pie, and about her indulging in a small glass of wine. By the time Vera falls asleep in the small bedroom of the suite, she allows herself to feel some hope that the next day—Black Friday—will be a happy one.

Unfortunately, Dad awakens with a case of sun poisoning that imprisons him in the hotel for the next few days. At first, Ma and Vera maintain their parallel schedules, only intersecting when they both need something from the hotel room. But by midday, Dad decides to disrupt this uneasy détente by speaking to Ma while Vera is in the nearby bathroom.

"You should try harder to talk to her," Dad whispers.

"She's always liked you better," Ma whines, sounding like

Vera's children when she denies either of them the "shotgun" position by making both share the backseat of the car.

As her parents' emotions become more intense, their voices rise, making it possible for Vera to hear every nuance of their conversation, even though the air conditioner in the suite roars like the iconic lion of MGM fame. Dad urges Ma to take advantage of his infirmity to bond with Vera, and Ma, in an unusual moment of conciliation, reluctantly agrees. And that is how Vera ends up spending Black Friday strolling the beach with her mother.

Ma and Vera walk side-by-side on the beach—the older and thinner woman with the darkening skin next to the taller, rounder, paler version Ma considers her defective doppelganger. Ma sees Vera's flawed life not as an indication of her failings as a mother but as a sign of Vera's failure to adhere to Ma's dictates and to meet her expectations. The two have the same eyes, nose, and overall facial structure, but Vera's refusal—or inability—to create an orderly existence or to assume a perfect façade for the world to admire results in Ma's hurt feelings and a deep-rooted alienation from her only daughter. Vera, knowing how Ma regards her, fears that this walk on the beach will end badly with Ma pushing her under a wave or cutting her artery with the sharp edge of a shell.

Silence—not the comfortable silence that Dad and Vera share, but the strained silence of strangers squeezed next to each other on a plane or of a man and woman on a blind date that should never have occurred—envelops Ma and Vera. Vera tries to lose herself in the songs of the gulls or the crashing of the waves, but she is too distracted by Ma's raised eyebrows, pursed lips, or occasional heaving of her shoulders—all signs of Ma's discontent with her daughter and life itself. By the time the beaming sun has moved higher in the sky, Vera is sweating from both heat and anxiety; her terry cloth cover-up feels heavy, as if it has fallen into the ocean and not adequately dried. Finally, as she and Ma reach the beach adjacent to one of the more elite and expensive hotels, Vera musters the courage to break the silence.

"Ma, do you remember how much fun we used to have on Black

Fridays?"

The sound of Vera's voice shocks Ma; she almost stumbles over a discarded bucket and shovel lying near a half-built castle in the sand. Then, regaining her physical and emotional balance, Ma retorts, "No, that was a long time ago."

"But, Ma, those days were so special. Don't you remember? You would always wake me up early on Black Friday, encouraging me to dress in an outfit I usually saved for a birthday or a religious holiday. You even let me wear your faux pearl circle pin and faux leather gloves. Remember how I wanted to wear my patent leather shoes with the tiniest of heels, but you—rightfully so—insisted we wear sensible shoes—flats with soft soles that would enable us to rush comfortably from table to table, store to store?"

Ma remains silent, although she seems to be listening to Vera's tale of the past.

"We always took the streetcar downtown, Ma, and you would spend the entire ride talking to me—chatting about the interesting people who walked along the crowded sidewalks; pointing out the grand Cathedral of Learning and explaining to me how you had contributed dimes to help build this structure that represented the mind and soul of the local university; sharing with me your memories of going to musical performances at the arena that looked like a metal igloo. Once in town, we entered Kaufmann's Department Store—you know, the one with the ornate golden clock above the doorway—and headed towards the men's section. You held my hand, Ma, so I would not get lost in the crowd."

Even now, decades later, Vera remembers the feel of Ma's skin around her palm and fingers; despite its roughness from so many hours of washing and cleaning, Ma's hand soothed Vera and let Vera know that her stern mother did have a soft side, even though she kept it hidden deep within her.

"After dropping off packages of undershirts and socks for Dad and school shirts for Harry at Dad's nearby optometric office, we would return to the store and let the fun part of the day begin. Ma, you knew how much I loved playing dress-up in your old clothes and in Grandma's early twentieth century dresses and hats, so you loaded the dressing room with glittery gowns and feathered hats that you would never ever buy and that I would never ever wear"— except, Vera thinks, in her fantasy world where she sometimes allowed herself to imagine being a princess surrounded by princely suitors and ladies-in-waiting.

Vera still speaks, but also indulges in moments of silence when she gets lost in her reverie—her more personal memories of past Black Fridays. She remembers the dressing room giving her the freedom to transform from the awkward, buck-toothed, too-tall-for-her-age young girl into a teacher, a debutante, a model, an executive's secretary (women did not become executives in the 1950s). She remembers Ma, the grim woman who rarely smiled as she intently washed, ironed, darned, cooked, cleaned, vacuumed, and performed all the other chores necessary to keep a house in order, relaxing on the chair in the dressing room, nodding her head and clapping her hands with approval as Vera donned one outfit after another. Ma would give Vera so many smiles and compliments that Vera actually believed that the right clothes and attitude might make her pretty. For a woman who felt uncomfortable with "once upon a time" and "happily ever after" stories, Ma seemed intent upon creating a fairy tale day for her daughter.

Vera did not even mind when Ma gathered all the never-to-be-bought garments and replaced them with the generic skirts, blouses with round collars, and cardigan sweaters that made her look like the six, seven, eight, nine, or ten-year-old she was. She did not sigh when Ma added some white and black knee socks to the mix. Instead, she concentrated on what came next: a cheeseburger and milkshake at the Milkshake Bar, a meal her "you cannot be too thin" mother usually did not condone.

"Ma, I know you remember the Milkshake Bar and then strolling past the majestic Warner Theatre that looked like a castle to the Jenkin's Arcade full of colorful stores already decorated for the holidays." Vera embraces the memories of how she and Ma spent hours window-shopping and pretending until the sun began to move closer to its nighttime hideaway.

By the time Dad joined them for dinner and Vera had licked the last bit of chocolate fudge cake off her plate, she was tired and ready for the curtain to come down on Black Friday. She had accumulated enough memories of laughter and love, she thought, to last her a lifetime.

Vera tells bits and pieces of these memories to Ma as they walk the beach, but she does not add that the next day, Ma would revert to her rigid routine—and that her mouth would again become a straight line, not the softer curved one of a smile. Vera would return to her family of plastic dolls, her card games with Grandma, and her television watching with Dad.

"Ma." Vera hates the tone of begging in her voice. "Ma, I know you must remember those special Black Fridays."

"Vera," Ma snaps, "I am too tired to relive the past—or a past you have created. What you have said sounds like foolishness—and I am not a foolish person."

Vera wants a wave to wash her away. She wants to bury herself in the sand or dig a hole that will take her all the way to China. Maybe the sun will melt her, or she will turn into a shell with a hard, protective outer layer. Ma either really does not remember—or chooses to forget.

Vera walks more slowly, copying the "turtle trudge" that had defined her high school years—head lowered into her neck, eyes focused on the ground. The hope for a re-capturing of the Black Friday exuberance of her youth leaves her; Vera feels empty and hollow. Then, Ma suddenly taps her shoulder and points.

"Look at those children over there, Vera. Look at how much fun they are having playing in the sand together. You used to have fun like that with your friends in the neighborhood."

Vera stares at Ma, convinced that the sun that has tanned her skin has also fried her brain. Maybe she has taken one of Dad's antihistamines by mistake and is having an allergic reaction to the medicine. Maybe Ma is on the verge of a stroke and, instead of looking at Ma with her mouth hanging open like that of a thirsty dog, Vera should be calling 911. Ma, oblivious to the shock her false memory has on Vera, continues walking.

Vera knows she should just let Ma's words go—let them be carried back to the ocean with the next large wave. But she cannot.

"Ma, I had no friends," Vera states. "Unless you count Oscar."

"Oscar?" questions Ma. "No, you had lots of friends, but no Oscar. I would remember someone with such an odd name."

Of course, Ma, who has deleted the magic of Black Fridays from her memory bank, does not remember Oscar. While Oscar was tangible, he was not human—only something Vera had invented during a long family drive to Niagara Falls.

Vera was about six years old when she, her parents, older brother, Harry, and paternal grandma embarked upon their road trip. Within the first thirty minutes of the drive, Harry had already managed to lean over Grandma, the human buffer seated between them, and put his freshly chewed gum into Vera's hair. Vera had tried to ignore him by drawing pictures of flowers and trees and stick people on her Magic Blackboard, but she soon tired of that activity. A game of "Twenty Questions" with Grandma ended after question four when Grandma's snores shook the backseat of the car. To amuse herself, Vera started fidgeting with the tissues in the Kleenex box, twisting and turning each piece into a different grotesque shape. Then, on a whim, she took a fresh tissue and secured only the tip of it in the closed window; the rest hung on the outside, blowing in the summer breeze.

Vera spent miles staring at that fragile tissue battling the unrelenting assaults of strong air caused by passing trucks and cars. With each new attack, the wind gobbled another piece of tissue. Soon, the tissue looked like a crudely designed piece of filigree or a glued collage of flakes from the mashed potato mix Ma sometimes used.

Recognizing the vulnerability of the tissue, Vera rolled down the window and gingerly placed the tattered tissue in her lap. She asked Ma if she would search her purse—that magical, seemingly bottomless bag that contained everything from candy to crayons, band aids to scissors—for a box. Without questioning her request, Ma gave Vera the box that usually held her pearl necklace; it became the home of Oscar, Vera's new best friend.

Oscar, safe within his box and a plastic bag for extra protection, joined Vera on the Maid of the Mist boat ride. He slept under her pillow in the motel room she shared with Grandma and Harry, and he watched with envy as Vera licked a triple-scoop cone of chocolate, vanilla, and strawberry ice cream. Once home, he lived in Vera's top dresser drawer. Vera's need to have a friend led her to share everything with Oscar: she confessed to him that she had enjoyed Linda's embarrassment when the popular girl had wet her pants in front of the class; she admitted that she hated gym class— a setting in which dodge balls attacked her and her legs got tangled up in her clumsy efforts to do a forward roll; she revealed that she only lip-synced in music class because even she could hear how out-of-tune her voice sounded.

And Oscar always listened without criticizing, teasing, or judging. Oscar became Vera's faithful journal, filling the human emptiness that consumed her.

Then, one day when Vera went to her dresser drawer to remove the box containing Oscar, she discovered an empty space. Ma, she had called, where is the box from my drawer? Oh, Ma had replied, I needed it for some old earrings. But what did you do with the tissue in it? a panicked Vera had asked. That piece of trash? Ma had responded. I tossed it in the garbage.

"Ma, you really don't remember Oscar, that tissue friend I made when we drove to Niagara Falls?" Vera asks Ma. She feels it is important for Ma to acknowledge this essential "friend" in her life, especially on this upsetting Black Friday beach walk.

After some contemplation, Ma replies, "I vaguely remember the trip—you and Harry arguing in the backseat and driving Grandma crazy. Didn't Dad have to stop the car so you could throw up by the side of the road?"

Vera shakes her head in despair and disappointment. To

discuss the past with Ma is as futile as trying to prevent a wave from reaching the shore.

The walk continues, ending only when Vera and Ma reach a part of the beach in which the sand has turned coarse; that is when they decide to turn back. Although a few white clouds move lazily across the sky and cool them, Vera yearns for an ice cream cone from the one vendor on the beach. But to have ice cream before dinner is going against the rules Ma established long ago when Vera was little: no snacking between meals. Vera does not even ask Ma if they can indulge.

By the time Vera and Ma reach their hotel, the tide has washed away their footprints, and the sun has almost finished its daily descent. The two enter the elevator in silence, eager to rejoin Dad who will, as always, lighten the heavy mother/daughter mood.

"How was your walk?" a hopeful Dad asks.

"Fine," Vera mumbles.

"Very pleasant," Ma agrees. "We had a good time reminiscing."

Ma's comment about the beach walk fills Vera with incredulity. Does Ma believe her assessment of the day, or is she trying to appease Dad with her alternate memory of the past hours? Vera bites her tongue—causing blood to fill her mouth—in an effort to remain quiet.

That night, Vera lies in her bed, tossing and turning, unable to fall asleep. What keeps her awake is not the cacophony of discordant notes emanating from the air conditioner, but is instead her memories of the day—and their jarring inconsistency with Ma's memories. She begins to wonder about the validity of her remembrances: Did those magical Black Fridays really occur, or does Vera only hope that they had occurred? Had her younger self been lonely enough to create a friend like Oscar, or are her memories of Oscar only reflective of her tendency to indulge in self-pity? Is Ma right—is anyone who looks back foolish? Vera grabs a tissue—a descendant of Oscar—to wipe the tears from her eyes.

Vera also wonders what other memories Ma has diluted or

deleted: the summer when four-year-old Vera gave Ma a daily "pedicure" with Q-tips and water; the backyard picnics with Ma's special egg salad sandwiches and—the only time Ma allowed this salty, fatty treat—chips; the visits to the children's room of the library where Ma introduced Vera to her favorite books, including her special "The Good Earth" by Pearl S. Buck; the phone call that Vera had been tapped for Phi Beta Kappa during her junior year that made Ma cry tears of joy; the later phone call that Vera had been named Teacher of the Year in her district, also causing Ma to weep with happiness; all the moments when Ma and Vera had connected, shared, and enjoyed each other. Vera cherishes these memories, but after the walk on the beach, she fears that these memories, like the family photo album Ma recently decided to burn in her apartment building's incinerator, no longer live within Ma.

Vera lies on her back, staring at the web-like cracks in the hotel room's ceiling, trying to understand the malleability of memory. Maybe people, even mothers and daughters, can experience the same moments in time, but have diverse or contradictory memories of those moments—or no memories at all. Maybe each memory has a different version, with no version being right or wrong—except in the mind and heart of the person remembering.

Eventually, Vera falls asleep, wrapping herself in her own memories. She promises herself that she will embrace these memories, even those not remembered by others, including Ma, or those perhaps enhanced by Vera's creative mind. Her memories, whether fact or fiction, will always remind her of who she was— and who she is. They will always give her a past, something she profoundly needs during a disappointing present and an uncertain future.

About the author:

Ronna Lynn Edelstein is a mother, avid reader, active theatregoer, and lifelong learner and teacher. She tries to find meaning and beauty in the world around her—and in those who inhabit it. As a part-time faculty member of the University of Pittsburgh's English Department, Ronna works as a consultant at the school's Writing Center. She also teaches Freshman Programs, a course that introduces students to the university and the city. Her work, both fiction and non-fiction, has appeared in the following: Dream Quest One (first place), First Line Anthology, Pulse: Voices from the Heart of Medicine, SLAB: Sound and Literary Artbook, Quality Women's Fiction, Ghoti Online Literary Magazine, and the Pittsburgh Post-Gazette and Washington Post, among others. Ronna thanks Scribes Valley for publishing "The Malleability of Memory," her eleventh story starring Vera.

IN MY DADDY'S SHOES
©2019 by Leslie Muzingo

Looking back, I guess the summer I was twenty-three was my favorite summer. I had me a job in a bookstore where I was paid a decent wage and not worked to death. This was no small thing as black girls just didn't get good cashier jobs in 1965. How did I rate? Maybe it was my smile—Momma always said I had movie star teeth—or maybe it was that Mr. Owner Man was my Daddy's white sergeant back in the Big War and promised to always help our folks out. Promised my Daddy as he died in Mr. Owner Man's arms down in some trench in France, and he's done things for our folks ever since then including give me a job in his store.

It doesn't matter how I got the job—I got it and was properly grateful too. Had me some nice clothes, some respectable men knocking at Momma's door asking for me, and also a prime place in the church choir. Then the summer of 1965 came around and I got me my first paid vacation.

We held a family meeting with lots of pie to decide where I should go. This was mostly an excuse for pie since we all knew I needed to visit Auntee Earnestine in Little Rock. No one from our Chicago family had seen her in eighteen years.

I was five, maybe six, when Auntee left Chicago to marry. We had a big dinner the night before she left and, being the youngest, I ran around like a spoiled injun while folks talked. Guess Auntee was the first to pay me any mind because I remember her pushing herself away from the table and announcing that she was going to tuck me in. Taking me to my room, she parked me in a big chair, my feet dangling, while she made my bed up clean. Before stripping me down, she got a basin full of cool water, some soap, and a towel.

First, she cleaned my face and body. Then she set me on the edge of the bed with orders to wait while she changed the water. I wasn't used to sitting around neked, not with four older brothers who might see what God commanded us to hide. I was tempted to jump up and run into the living room and show everyone how she'd left me with no clothes to wear. Before I could sin, Auntee Earnestine was back with fresh water which she used to bath my feet. She soaked them first, and while they soaked, she rubbed my legs into feeling like warm jelly. Then, once my feet were clean, she dried them hard with the rough towel, rubbing away both the water's chill and my last flicker of anger and leaving nothing but a child who wanted her bed.

"Always stay clean and nice, Maisie," she said, her voice like a low caress.

After tucking me in she turned off the light and sang softly until she thought I was asleep. My last view of her was a shape in the doorway as she left, not just for the night, but to move away, and to never return. I remember wanting to reach out for a hug, a kiss, a touch, but she'd tranquilized me with her song. I was asleep before she could darken my room by shutting the door.

None of us had seen her since, nor had we met her husband or any of the children that came later. Jimmy made it too hard to travel. "Oh, Jimmy Crow," Momma would sing with her hand on her big hip, "he makes you stay when you want to go, oh Jimmy! Jimmy Crow, let me, let me go!" Sometimes Momma would dance when she'd sing. The madder she was that travel was so hard when you had no car and had five little kids, the more she'd sing. As we got older, Momma got bigger and her dance got fiercer, and before long she was more jiggle than dance. The boys wanted to buy the Green Book of Travel that would've told us where Negros could go, but Momma wasn't risking putting her children in danger. By the time we became adults us kids all agreed that even if there'd been public bathrooms and lunch counters that Momma could'a used on the long trip, she'd never have fit in the seats on the bus no how.

Besides, it was me, not Momma, who was going off to see Auntee. Mr. Lincoln freed the slaves, but it was Mr. Johnson who made it possible for us to go places! No more Jim Crow! Praise Jesus for 1965! Now we could finally pee in the same toilet and drink outta the same glass as everyone else, but I had too much to be happy about to be bitter. My brother's wives, none who'd even met Aunt Earnestine, had sifted through their finery and contributed their best gloves, hats, shirt waists and everything else I could wish for to look extra special nice. Mama had double starched and packed my clothes. Mr. President had signed the law almost a year ago anyways—I just never expected to have the time off from work to go anywhere. Not only did I have a paid vacation, but Mr. Owner Man gave me a stack of comic books and a mess of candy to give my little cousins. No Princess on a diplomatic tour was as ready to impress as I, nor was there a debutante with any more reason to have her heart a-flutter. I was traveling! It was a miracle, and it was happening to me!

On the ride out of Chicago I sat three seats back on the side facing west. With the sunshine warming my face, I was ready to greet everyone with a proud smile of hello. Didn't even occur to me that without Jim Crow white peoples wouldn't ride and that most black folks either had a car or were too poor to pay the fare. Or maybe it was just that it was so dang hot for folks to use the bus. I dunno.

It was gonna take some time for white folks and black folks to get used to one another, but I didn't know that yet. The only white person I knew was Mr. Owner Man who lived in a brick house with a white fence and flowers in his yard. He took us to his house once for Father's Day which seemed to make his wife mad.

Funny, for the longest time I thought all white folks lived in brick houses with white fences and had beautiful flowers growing in their yards. I wasn't seeing any of them in the tenement where I lived, and they had to live somewhere. They sure weren't on the bus that day.

The sun was a fireball against the flat river land when we pulled into Keokuk. As the sun went down, so did my smile, and I leaned against the window to nap.

It's odd how there was no white peoples and then as soon as I closed my eyes there were five of them. I felt a body plop next to me and heard a soft giggle, so I opened my eyes and bouncing on the seat beside me was the prettiest little white child I'd ever seen. She giggled again when she saw me looking at her and then clapped her tiny hands over her mouth. Her huge blue eyes laughed and begged for me to tickle her, but I had better sense. "What's your name?" I asked.

Lifting her hands off one corner of her mouth she whispered, "Jilly!" before pressing her hands down on her lips as if she feared more words might escape.

Her hair looked like spun gold. Clutching my pocketbook kept my hands busy so I wouldn't touch it. "Miss Jilly, do you travel often?" I asked.

The tiny hands flew away, and Jilly squealed. "No! Never! This is the very first time!" The child then leaped up and ran back to her mother. By discretely turning my body, I could see Jilly's mother in the shadows. There were four other unusually quiet children with the woman but no grown folk.

Jilly visited me several times that evening. Always giggling, she ran up and down the aisle until the bus driver made her stop. Even his scolding did not kill her joy. Later she pulled an older sister by the hand to meet me. "She's Sarah," Jilly announced.

Sarah nodded politely. "I'm sorry she's bothering you, Miss."

Miss!

"She's just so happy, and Momma..."

Momma!

"...says if she's not hurting anything to leave her be. Hope she's not bothering you too much."

I smiled at Sarah, and she smiled back. "I like talking to her, and to you too,"

At midnight we pulled into St. Louis for a six-hour layover. This was the scary part of the trip. Jim Crow had never been bad in Chicago except that it kept us from traveling. Those with a car could always make a trip if they were ready for a little hardship like packing their own food and using the woods for their necessaries when there weren't any friendly facilities. But folks like us with no car were stranded. We could travel by bus to some places, but St. Louis was a hard town. Momma had given me strict instructions that under no circumstances should I leave the bus station. She said, "Don't be fooled into thinking that Jim Crow is dead in St. Louie. Signing a law don't mean squat. No matter what, chile, don't you leave that bus station for so much as to buy a stick of gum—you hear me?" I'd already heard about St. Louis; some of the girls in the choir were talking after practice. What they said frightened me. I heard my Momma now—loud and clear.

The bus station was huge. I started to find me a quiet spot by myself until I remembered that terrible things happened to girls that went off alone into corners. I saw the white woman and her five children and reckoned I'd just sit close by them.

Jilly hugged my leg when she saw me. Her mother didn't seem to care. I started to offer Jilly some of my food but decided that would be akin to a stranger offering a child candy, and I didn't want no one calling no police, especially in St. Louis. I decided I'd wait to eat till Jilly ate with her family.

An hour went by. Then another. And another. None of those white folks ate or drank nothing but water. Then I hear Jilly cry out, "I got to go pee!"

Sarah, like a little momma, took Jilly's hand and they went to the restroom. They immediately came back. Sarah whispered something in her mother's ear which seemed to make the woman angry. "I can't believe you'd ask me for money for that!" It was the first words I'd heard from the woman, and the hard sound shocked me when compared to the silly sounds that came from Jilly or the soothing tones Sarah made.

Sarah seemed subdued by her mother's harshness, but Jilly was going as if on batteries. The two girls turned to go back to the bathroom, and their mother gestured to the teenage daughter to go too. Curious, I had to see what caused such a ruckus, so I gathered my things and followed them.

I entered the bathroom just in time to see Jilly crawling under the bathroom door. Her skimpy pink shift acted as a mop and was picking up dirt, dust, filth, and crud of every kind imaginable, and her panties were a-glow for all of us to see. Sarah was across the way crawling under another stall, and it was the same story there except Sarah had a big ole hole in her underwear. The older sister stood leaning up against a sink with her arms tightly crossed as if she were angry with the world.

I wasn't having this. "You girls get up offa that floor this minute!"

That's when the three children started talking at once.

"But I gotta pee!"

"The toilets take a dime!"

"I'm so embarrassed I could die."

"We can't let her wet herself—we don't have clean clothes."

"Why does this always happen to me?"

Giggles. "I gotta pee NOW."

"Jilly, if you wet yourself so help me, I'll tan your butt!"

"Don't tell her that. You know you won't."

"Can I please go pee?"

"Just get off the floor now! Back up and come out. I have a dime!" I was about to explode—the very idea of children crawling on the bus station floor where winos, women winos anyway, had probably dribbled urine made bile rise in my throat. Their childish heads would be next to the vile toilet which, if it were anything like the rest of the station, was sure to be infested with crawling bugs of every kind. I couldn't take it another second; I reached down and pulled Jilly's legs to drag her back to safety. "Wee!" she cried as if she were on some carnival ride. "Do it again!"

Sarah managed to get out of from under the toilet door on her own. With a shaking hand, I dug in my purse and pulled out a dime and put it in the slot. The door opened, and in went Jilly, yanking down her panties as she ran. On the floor beside the commode lay used hygiene products. It was everything I could do to maintain my composure and not throw up.

After the three girls had used the facilities, I filled a sink with water and began cleaning Jilly. "Oh, that feels nice!" she slurred, her eyelids falling to half-mast. Although Sarah didn't really need my help, she welcomed the attention. So, while helping Sarah clean up, I gave them all my Auntee Earnestine's "always keep yourself clean" lecture.

Becky, the teenager, was unimpressed. "That's easy for you to say. Just look at you. I bet you never had to crawl under a toilet to pee."

I could've said a lot of things right then, but instead I just agreed with her. "Becky, you're right. I never did. Why wouldn't your Momma give you the dime?"

That's when Becky started sobbing and talking at the same time. It was hard for me to understand all that she said, but what was hardest to take in was the realization that not all white folks had a brick house with a white fence and flowers in the yard.

I felt I was paying a small price for what I'd learned by giving Becky enough dimes for their journey. I also put a ten-dollar bill into her hand. "Tell your Mother you found it on the floor. But don't find it until later. You understand me?" The girl nodded. She's been slipped money before, I thought.

Once alone in the restroom, I went through the ritual of cleaning myself as if it were a sacrament. I cleaned the basin before running it full of fresh water so that I could wash my face, hands, and neck. The cool water on my arms restored my soul; when I thought of how much I had, I knew that my cup truly runneth over. Yes, a white man had called me "nigger" that morning when I went to the store to fetch coffee for breakfast, but his words meant little at the time because I was excited about my trip. Now his words meant even less.

Upon leaving the restroom I bustled over to the family. The mother looked alarmed, so I quickly explained that I was visiting my Auntee and had candy bars for her children but that I suddenly remembered that her son was a diabetic. "I can't take this candy into the house, and it would be a shame to throw it away. Would you like it for your children?"

No one slept but Jilly, and at the mention of the gift of candy the rest of the children all began speaking at once. "Quiet!" their mother hissed. "Whoever wakes her doesn't get any!"

Silence.

"Thank you, Miss..."

"Maisie."

"Thank you, Miss Maisie. That is very kind of you."

I handed her the bag of candy. "There are a few comic books in there too. My boss gave them to me for my cousins. I guess he didn't realize that he'd given me duplicates. But I'm glad to pass them on to your children if you'll allow them to have them."

"That's very kind of you."

"Not at all. I hope it brings them some pleasure and allows you to get a little rest."

As I walked away, I expected to hear the rip of paper floating behind me. Instead, I overheard soft whines of, "but Momma!" Taking my seat, I saw that the mother was breaking one candy bar into pieces and giving each child a small portion. The rest she put in her purse.

The sun came up early, or so it seemed to me. I know it hadn't been getting light outside at five a.m. back in Chicago. I gathered my things and walked where I thought it safest. It was still a long ride to Little Rock, and I needed exercise. Later I wondered if God had turned on the sun a bit early that morning, so I'd see Becky outside.

I was by the doors where the buses pulled in when I saw her. She had the comic books I'd given them pressed up against her chest, and she was crying. Looked like she had good reason for tears as she was surrounded by four black teenage boys. Although they were probably younger than Becky, they were bigger, and I could tell at a glance that this was more than boys teasing a girl. One boy grabbed Becky's arm and through the glass door I watched his mouth shape a menacing laugh when she pulled away. His eyes narrowed, and he nodded to his friends. Suddenly it was like a black spider was attacking the girl with one spider leg covering her mouth and the rest of the spider ripping at her clothes and pushing her up against the wall.

"No matter what, chile, don't you leave that bus station for so much as to buy a stick of gum—you hear me?" Momma's words came back to me like a commandment, but this was a commandment I was going to break, so help me God! I threw my things down and flung open the door. "Get off her! Now! Her momma called the police, so you better run if you know what's good for you!"

The three accomplices froze. The ringleader laughed. "She's bluffing!"

For what seemed like forever, the other three boys stood completely still. I thought maybe time was frozen until one of the boys wiped sweat from his face. "Maybe it's a bluff and maybe it ain't. I can't risk it. They'll send me up for sure." He turned and ran.

Everything went fast then. The tallest boy looked down into my eyes and I saw fear in his dilated pupils. I refused to look away, and he began to shake. "Ezra, wait for me!" he called after the running figure.

"I'm with you, brother!" said the third boy. The two of them ran like rabbits after the first.

The ringleader was left. He stuck his chin in the air. "You don't scare me. Maybe I do you next, huh?"

I've always been a passive sort of girl. I have four older brothers who treated me like a princess. Being pretty helps in life because kids in school don't pick on you. This must've been my first physical confrontation. Seeing that poor white girl slide to the sidewalk with her clothes torn and with comics falling around her like a bad joke forced me to make up for lost time, I guess. It was like something inside of me caught on fire.

I took me three long steps to be up next to the boy—he didn't seem so fierce now—and those three steps helped me catch my rhythm, for as soon as I completed step three my right arm came up and slapped his face with such a POP that it knocked him up against the wall. Before he could react, I slapped him again and again. It didn't take more than a few of those strong slaps before his nose was bloody and the boy was crying.

Becky stood up.

"You want to hit him?" I asked.

She shook her head. "I want to cut him," she said.

"Please! Please let me go!" the boy cried.

Becky reached in her pocket. "Cut him up good."

"Jesus! Help me!" the boy sank to the ground.

Becky pulled out a comb. "But all I've got is this damn comb, so I guess I'll kick him instead." She gave the boy a hard kick in the ribs. "Peed on yourself, didn't you?" she jeered. "And you peed on my comic books. Now you owe me for these comic books. Pay up. Now."

With a shaking hand, the boy pulled out his wallet and opened it. "I don't have much," he whimpered.

Becky grabbed the wallet and took out the money. "Now you have nothing." Becky dropped the wallet on the ground and looked at me. "Let's go before someone steals your stuff."

As we entered the station I turned back and looked at the boy. He was silently weeping. I had no sympathy for him. I turned back to Becky and put my arm around her. "You okay?" I asked.

She shrugged my arm away. "Sure." She looked at me with eyes too old for her years. "Thanks for your help."

I wasn't insulted by her rebuff. Becky didn't want pity, and I couldn't wash away her dirt. "What were you doing out there?" I asked as I picked up my bags.

The girl closed her eyes as she turned to face me. She took a deep breath before opening them, and her chin went up an inch before she spoke. "I guess you have a right to know, not because you helped me but because they were your comic books. I was trying to sell them. If we don't get some money before we get to Aunt Darlene's house, then she will take one of us. "Off Mama's hands," is how she said it. She'll either take Jilly so at least one of us is brought up right, or me since I was old enough to do some work." Becky looked away. It struck me then that she was more ashamed of her poverty than standing in the bus station in a shirt torn enough that her young bosom showed.

Old age reached too soon was foreshadowed in that young girl's eyes and upturned chin. "She's not getting Jilly. She's not hurting our baby."

Before I knew it, I was telling her about Mr. Owner Man and how he'd helped us and that I was gonna ask him to help Becky and her family.

"Why would he help us?" Becky shook her head like she thought I was out of my mind.

"He'll help you." I looked at the station clock. I had twenty minutes before my bus left. "Come on," I said. "We gotta find a pay phone."

Becky's family were going to Kansas City and their bus didn't leave till seven, so that would at least buy a little time. I got on the phone and placed a collect call to Mr. Owner Man. Funny, I'd been calling him that in my mind so long that I stumbled over his real name when I had to give it to the operator.

I prayed he would answer the phone. His wife was nice, but I could count on the third degree if she answered. Momma once told me that the woman was barren, but I didn't know why that would make her nasty to me. Luckily, he answered the phone and accepted the charges without hesitating.

"What is it, Maisie? Are you all right?" there was concern in his voice.

"Yes sir, I am, but I have to tell you about someone quick before my bus leaves. Please just let me talk for a bit." So, Mr. Owner

Man listened as I told him how much our whole family appreciated his help these past twenty years. Then I told him about this family. I wanted him to hear Jilly's giggle and see Sarah's solemn eyes. What did it say about two boys who never left their mother's side? Were they protecting her or themselves? And Becky—how many teenage girls would risk rape to sell comic books to help out the family? The mother was confused—who wouldn't be with her husband killed in the war?

"Your mother wasn't," he said.

"My momma had you."

That settled it. I'd keep my job, but that was all we'd count on Mr. Owner Man to do for us. He'd start helping Becky and her family instead.

"Tell Becky I'll be sending them money through Western Union," he instructed.

"You tell Becky. I've got to go. Thank you. Thank you for everything."

I handed the phone to Becky, grabbed my bags, and ran out the door. I had time to gobble my lunch and to get myself comfortable before the driver sank into his seat. He then went over a checklist and closed the door. He started to pull out when suddenly there was a poundin' on the bus door. He opened it, and in dashed Becky's momma. Her eyes quickly found me, and she flew to me despite the bus driver's hollering.

The woman said nothing. She just looked at my face as if she were trying to memorize me, and then she hugged me tight. Before I could hug her back, she'd let go and was flying down the bus steps. The bus driver gave her a few more yells as she ran away, shook his head, and pulled out of the station.

The visit with Aunt Earnestine was wonderful. I'd kept a few comic books back for her children, but they weren't really interested in them; they wanted to get to know their cousin from Chicago. I don't think I ever again ate as much pie!

I worked in the bookstore for five more years. I decided to quit when my wedding plans began taking up too much of my time. I'd have quit once I was married anyway.

On my last night, when we were locking up, Mr. Owner-Man says, "Maisie, come into my office. I want you to help me with something."

I'd never gone into Mr. Owner Man's office all that time I worked for him. I'd walk past sometimes and see him a-sitting at a desk cluttered with pictures in frames. Never knew how the man got anything done there were so many pictures on that desk. I always figgered they were of his wife.

We entered his office together. "I know you have a lot to do," he said, "but I was hoping you could help me rearrange these pictures."

I walked over to the desk and for the first time saw that the pictures were of me and my brothers. There were some of Momma too with all of us together. The pictures started back from when I was about five years old and continued through each of my brothers' weddings.

"I want you to arrange these pictures on the shelf against the wall."

I noticed then that the shelf was lighted. I mentioned this to him. He only smiled.

"Spread the pictures out so they take up the whole shelf. I plan to add to this collection for years to come, and that way I can easily make room for more pictures. The next one I hope to get is one you send me taken at your wedding. Anyway, I need space on my desk for some other pictures."

He opened a drawer and took out a framed photograph. He held it out to me. I gasped when I saw the picture; there was Jilly laughing up at me. She was ten years old now, but she had the same joyful eyes. Sarah, now thirteen, was still little Momma standing protectively next to her. The boys each had an arm linked in with their Momma's—they were her knights to defend her against the world. But it was Becky's face that warmed my heart. Her big open smile was so different from the bitter teenager I'd met at the bus station. It was as if someone had erased her pain and drawn on her face a new life.

I turned to Mr. Owner-Man—Jim McCleery—and was suddenly flooded with the realization of how much he'd done for my family over the years. They had always seemed like little things at the time, yet now I knew we'd never have made it without him. Other than my hurried thank you over the phone from St. Louis, I'd never thanked him properly for anything. I thought he did it as a chore because of my Daddy, but for the first time I realized he had stepped into my Daddy's shoes, and he wore those shoes all those years because he liked the way they fit. There was only one way to repay him.

"Since you'll be walking me down the aisle you'll be in the pictures, so of course you'll get one. You will take my Daddy's place and walk me down, won't you?"

I saw the joy of Jilly in his eyes when he took my hand.

About the author:

Leslie Muzingo grew up in Iowa but relocated to the Deep South years ago. She spends her summers on Prince Edward Island and finds great similarities between PEI and the Iowa of her youth. Her work has been published by *Pink Panther Magazine, Ink in Thirds, Two Sisters Writing, Mother's Milk Books, Darkhouse Books, Literary Mama, Iowa State Writer's Guild,* among others. She considers herself an emerging writer. Her emergence is a slow one as she has many joys and interests, and there are only so many hours in a day. Leslie can be found on Goodreads, Amazon's Authors, and under the handle of Sootfoot5 on Twitter.

DEVILED EGGS
©2019 by John Francis Istel

"Put on some clothes. I'm not your mother, for god's sake," Melanie hisses, backing toward the kitchen door.

Actually, Jim isn't completely naked—a Nike wristband circles each forearm, a bright orange life preserver cinches tight across his chest, and a two-foot long tattoo of Neptune's trident runs from his belly button up to his neck, the tines cradling his chin. Otherwise, in the important places, he is naked as a newborn.

Jim charges at her, chasing Melanie around the kitchen island for the third time. When she heads for the back door, he is but a few slippery feet behind and is determined to prevent her escape. As he patters by the counter, however, he almost topples over a platter of deviled eggs. Luckily, he catches the tray, steadies it, and briefly studies the way the whites, yellows, and burnt orange of the paprika radiate from light to dark.

The eggs, intended for the brunch Melanie had planned for her husband, Chris, are arranged in concentric circles. Jim knows a mandala worth eating when he sees it. He had only scarfed down a few fistfuls of KiX cereal earlier in the morning, after he'd sharpened his scissors, untwisted a dozen coat hangers, and gulped down three cans of Red Bull. These eggs are too tempting.

Jim meditates on life's natural struggle between the physical— as exemplified by the egg yolk clinging to the roof of his mouth, and the ephemeral—as represented by the now broken circle of appetizers. He remembers Melanie fits into this cosmic conflict somehow, but when he looks up, she has scampered out the door into her sunny Connecticut suburban backyard.

Jim understands Hobbes though he doesn't recall reading him. He accepts that human beings bray through the world in a constant state of conflict, condemned to lives inevitably "solitary, poor, nasty, brutish and short." One second a body could be standing near, rolling a smoke, full of limbs and normal protrusions. The next second, that body could be missing a head, just like in World of Warcraft, which he would be playing on his old Dell desktop if he hadn't been sent on this mission.

Jim's fingers twitch over the remaining eggs as if they are flicking lint off a crisply pressed uniform. Meanwhile, Melanie scurries around outside on the back patio, desperate for a weapon of self-defense.

After Jim wolfs down his fourth deviled egg, he feels woozy. As he tries to chew a fifth, his tongue turns into a desert. He wheels to the sink and spits out what tastes like an Iraqi sandstorm, and then wrenches on the cold water and sticks his mouth under the faucet, head sideways, face toward the large plate glass window. From this vantage, his dreamy blue eyes catch Melanie zigzagging around the backyard like a concussed soldier struggling in retreat from a fire fight. He sees her hop over a fifty-foot dog leash, kick away a Bill Clinton doll chew toy, and duck under a double clothesline. As she zeroes in on the pre-formed plastic tool shed, her dirty blonde pigtails keep time like windshield wipers.

Remembering his task at hand, Jim bolts outside, leaving the water running in the kitchen sink. Melanie freezes when she hears the screen door bang. She turns and now questions why she was scared of this crazy, naked man in her yard on an otherwise wondrously warm early summer June morning.

Ten minutes earlier, when Melanie had first heard the front door slam open, she expected her husband to come jogging in. She'd prepared brunch in yoga pants because Chris seemed to like peeling them off her before gnawing at her slender neck like a vampire. But when Chris disappeared with the dogs at the crack of dawn, without so much as a peck or a pinch, she changed into her Banana Republic shorts. Chris never took the dogs on two-hour walks. She padded out to the front entry only to find Jim, their crazy tenant from above the garage, offering a little hop and a "Ta-Da!" as if surprising her at a birthday party.

Melanie's every rational thought dizzied and scrambled as images of the various parts of Jim's naked body crowded her vision. She panicked. His jazz hands flashed back and forth as he tried to shush her cries of "Get out" and "Get out now." His scraggly long hair bounced around his sweating, shining face, framing his droopy mustache, his queer ponytail tied like a pirate's with a black ribbon. Finally, Melanie's gaze grounded on his schlong, wagging like a slobbery dog's tongue.

"Shhhh. I'm not here to rape or pillage," Jim tried to reassure her. But at the sound of those words, as if the P's in rape and pillage were jet propellant, Melanie rocketed away toward the kitchen.

As they ran around the house in circles—through the living room, down the short hall to the den, into the chintzed and forlorn dining room and back through the kitchen to start all over again—Melanie realized how many chores her husband hadn't finished. He hadn't watered the lawn in a week or sprayed the driveway with herbicide and so dandelions were sprouting along the garage entrance. He forgot to buy the pimento-less olives she liked or take Kitty to the vet. He hadn't finished the fence so their Springer spaniels, named Rabbit and Goat, still had to be leashed up outside. It was as if in their eighth year of marriage he had gone on sabbatical.

"If maybes were babies..." Melanie thought, "I have enough to stock an orphanage." Maybe...Chris wasn't ready to be a dad though he'd already bought an entire Yankees infant outfit. Maybe...Chris knew she'd been lying about the digital basal thermometer's readings so she could limit when they had sex. Maybe...Chris found out how off-the-charts fertile she was this weekend. Maybe...Chris was just worn down since he started working so late that even the KFC was closed when he got off the train, and she'd throw some frozen food in the microwave. Maybe...she needed better lingerie. Maybe...he wanted her to earn more than the lousy "honorarium" she got from the 4H Club afterschool program where she volunteered. Maybe...Chris was far younger emotionally than the four and a half physical years she had on him. Maybe...Chris was the baby.

His recent lapses of judgment sure were doozies. He still hadn't apologized to their dogwalker's parents for somehow breaking the teenager's ankle while driving her home ten days ago though the car remained unscathed or scratched. "A severe swerve," was all she could piece out from his story. Chris also neglected to give Tina's parents their insurance information. The poor girl's father had called three times last week. Maybe that's why he's taking so long dropping off the darn dogs at her house for the weekend.

Clearly, Chris's most heinous mistake was Jim, who, from Melanie's vantage on the patio, now looks to be gargling in her kitchen sink. Chris promised to evict him from the apartment above the garage months ago. The list of grievances was long. The man terrified their neighbors' little twin girls by yelling, "Cootchy-cootchy-coo" while waggling his fingers through his own beard. He left brown paper bags of garbage on the curb instead of placing them in the new Home Depot containers she'd bought. He blasted air horns and sang "Tequila" during hockey season whenever the Rangers scored. The man was clearly disturbed. But the unforgiveable part was they hadn't seen a dime of rent since the initial security deposit, a Veterans' Administration check for $450 that Jim signed over to them.

Jim was the first and only tenant Chris interviewed after he converted the garage loft space into an apartment—the only house improvement he ever relished. He spent so much time picking out bedspreads and curtains and throw rugs that Melanie wondered why he hadn't shown such dedication after they closed on their own house. During one of many arguments about in-vitro versus adoption, she told him, "If you can't love anything but that apartment so much why don't you move into it." Then she slammed the bathroom door and spent thirty minutes or so cleaning and sterilizing every surface of the tiles, scrubbing every inch of her body, until she had regained enough breath to reenter her marriage.

Chris left every weekday on the 7:27 for Manhattan, abdicating responsibility for Jim to Melanie. A couple months back two Darien police officers brought Jim home in handcuffs, marched him up the blue slate path to the front door, and asked Melanie who the man's mother was.

"I don't know who his mother is."

"Aren't you this man's mother?"

"Of course she is, I told you already," Jim said, blinking his sad tea-bag eyes to indicate his wish for her complicity.

"He claims you've adopted him," said the younger, snappy officer with the Brillo hair and Lou Ferragamo eyes. "He was caught trespassing in the mall."

"I thought malls were public," Melanie said, fighting a desperate urge to close the door. It was after 7:30 on a Tuesday evening, she remembered. Chris should have been home to deal with such legal intricacies.

"He was in the security guard lounge area, ma'am. Strictly off limits."

"I needed help," Jim said, looking down at his sandals.

"He was using the toilet," Officer Lou said.

Melanie watched the town policemen watching her. "Surely that's not a crime..."

"Well, he wasn't using it in a traditional way."

Jim stood straighter and affirmed, "It's much more traditional than you might think, I'm afraid, especially in Fallujah."

Melanie's protective fallback grace and Episcopalian manners went into full retreat. She started to offer them a glass of water, but realized that would be awkward. She wanted to slam the door, grab Rabbit and Goat, and hide in the master bedroom. She peeped over the cops' shoulders to see if anyone across the street in the Jorgenson's house was watching.

"I have two large dogs, they're like small children, see, and I don't know if..."

"We'll release him to your supervision. Just see he stays out of trouble," said the short Danny DeVito officer as he began unfastening the cuffs. Melanie realized she just missed the chance to have him arrested.

Melanie kept nodding, though she didn't understand what they were saying about release protocols and court appearances. She did notice Jim's grin, his teeth scraggly like duckpins. The officers waddled back to the curb, opened the doors of their cruiser, and, as if choreographed, in one motion bent into the front seats, lowered their sunglasses, and slammed the doors.

Melanie turned to see Jim blow her a kiss as he headed back to the garage apartment rubbing his wrists.

"Hey, Jim. Rent's due," she managed to call out. It was all she could think to say whenever she saw him.

"You know, Melanie," he called out. "I've sacrificed a lot for my country, but I'm forever in your debt."

Any relief Melanie feels by her escape to the backyard turns to dismay as the heat of the midday sun on the patio slate burns the soles of her bare feet. She hops back and forth like waiting to return serve in a mixed doubles match. Melanie understands the gravity of her situation when she sees Jim's face disappear from the window over the kitchen sink. She feels a wave of fear and knows she needs to be armed. She lurches toward the tool shed to open the door. Maybe she can lock herself inside?

Instead, she discovers that Chris has installed a gym lock on the latch. Melanie herself insisted that the shed's tools stored were a menace to the neighborhood's children. The Jorgenson's little Sally could decide to pin the tail on a donkey with a nail gun. Or her brother, mini Mike, might want to play rock-paper-scissors with a chainsaw. She'd never thought of asking Chris for the lock's combination.

Cornered, Melanie grimly wheels around to face her foe. For a second, he seems to have disappeared. She almost laughs when she spots Jim prone on his stomach, doing an infantry crawl across the patio toward her. He starts to slide and elbow his way across the wet, newly watered lawn. About ten feet away, he jumps up into a karate stance, pleased to see his prey stationary. He edges himself closer like an inchworm, wriggling his wide toes in the grass, scrunching up his bare feet, and then pushing his heels closer. His life preserver glows a hotter orange as the high noon air raid siren wails.

Melanie notices the garden hose loosely coiled to her left. Hells bells, she thinks. She catapults herself down on it like a paratrooper falling to earth and in one motion rolls over, twists the nozzle on, and guns Jim hard, in the nuts. The power of the spray and the short distance has its effect. His eyes shrink to the size of a squirrel's as he tries to cover himself and slowly retreat backwards. As his bare feet give way in the saturated grass, Jim reaches out to Melanie as if she will save him. He falls, his head smashing backward on the expensive garden path stone that Chris installed last year so he wouldn't ruin the lawn on his infrequent trips to the shed. Jim's eyes roll up, and he lets out a little "oomph," although he is probably dead before Melanie hears it.

She doesn't know the danger has passed and keeps spraying, mesmerized by the way the water makes Jim's flesh ripple, how his penis flaps like a bell clapper if she aims just right.

Chris should be home any second, she thinks, any second. A dog-less weekend. She had no idea that Rabbit and Goat irked Chris so much, no idea that a romantic stay-cation would preclude her pets. They had agreed on 11:30 for brunch. With the dogs safely kenneled at Tina's, they were supposed to spend time patching everything up around the house. She'd prepared his favorites—the Scottish eggs, cantaloupe canoes, bacon lightly fried, and a pitcher of spicy Cajun Bloody Marys. But oddly he hadn't texted to say he'd be late. Chris was supercilious about keeping the world updated. He'd Tweet the locations of speed traps. Instagram the line at Dunkin' Donuts. Take a pic of his biceps at the gym and send it to Melanie on Snapchat.

Melanie relaxes her grip on the hose after she feels her hand go numb. She must have been spraying with all her might for hours. The hose drips on her forearm and she feels how soggy she's become from her Xena-like roll in the grass. She stands and smooths her khaki shorts and spots grass stains on her A&P League softball jersey.

She listens to the highway cars, all motoring somewhere this weekend, and she realizes how inured she is to living on the other side of a wall from I-95. There are no other discernable sounds, except her breathing through her nose, which feels hot like she is snorting steam and her upper lip begins to sting. She steps toward Jim's body and notices a Frisbee-sized pool of blood in the grass by his left ear.

He is a very large man—he could have hurt her in so many ways, she thinks. He isn't that young either, probably closer to 40 than she is, though he acts like he is right out of college. Her first thought: How awful and old must I look to be mistaken by those cops for this man's mother? Then the notion that he is dead, and naked, and in her backyard, and that she made him dead, if dead he is, mushrooms in her mind. Melanie starts to hyperventilate. She reaches for the roll of Tums in her shorts pocket and fears she might pass out, which is exactly the last thought she has before she does.

The crime-scene tableau is as lurid as anything the town of Darien has witnessed. A dead half-naked man, a comatose woman on top of him, a missing husband, water running in the kitchen sink. As the police tiptoe around the yard and unspool yellow tape, the neighbors gather at the foot of the drive, summoned as much by the sound of the walkie talkies as from the police cars and ambulance.

Two states away, Chris drives a pickup truck. He is approaching the Vince Lombardi Rest Area on I-95 South in New Jersey, heading to the Arizona-Mexico border. A teenage girl, too young to vote but old enough not to make Chris a criminal, sits in the cab's passenger seat, her foot, in a cast, up on the dashboard.

Chris knows he isn't taking a particularly courageous way out of his marriage, but he's flatters himself with the audacity of his plan. He replays the perfection of his planning as they roll south. The dogs? Safe with Tina's parents, who will find good homes for them. Or maybe they'll keep the spaniels because they'll have their daughter's empty room and an emotional void to fill. Will they paint over her Goth graffiti? Throw away her safety pins and henna? Her ripped t-shirts and black Converse high tops? The dogs are probably better company than the child they spawned, he thinks. Yes. They'll keep the dogs.

As for the disappearance of their daughter? Well, that grief—or guilt—may never die as long as they live. He looks over at Tina, oblivious, smoking a Newport, her white v-neck undershirt's sleeves rolled up, the needle pricks still visible on the tattoo of a snarling German shepherd she had inked on her upper arm yesterday. Chris smiles to himself. Tina couldn't wait to escape, so unless she suddenly gets homesick, her parents, Fred and Jo, will have to live with the assumption that their teen was murdered by the same schizophrenic, Iraqi war-traumatized, highly disturbed soldier that killed his wife. By this evening, Chris figures, the police will find the tacky naked sexts of Tina and Melanie that Chris planted in a file folder deep on Jim's hard drive. And his own vanishing? Who else but the jealous vet would have a motive to erase Chris from the face of the earth? Damn. What a plan.

Like most men, the enormity of the facts that Chris does not know vastly outweighs those that he assumes he does. He refuses to submit to ambiguities, to maybes. Chris gloms onto data, details, specifics, charts and surveys, even if the underlying truths are mythical. For example, he has no inkling that he laid the wrong, slippery side of the slate down in his backyard.

Furthermore, he forgot how fierce his wife was with a gun in her hand, even if he'd only seen her win Carnival prizes by firing water into a clown's mouth until she was first to make the bright balloon, looming over the Bozo's garish head, like a brilliant idea, explode. Chris, like so many men, drives federal highways on cruise control, clueless.

By the time he crosses into Maryland, Chris does not know that Melanie is alive, breathing through a tube, unconscious, hospitalized, and heavily sedated, but unbutchered. Prognosis? Full recovery within several days. Fact is, Chris doesn't know that the only victim is the man he'd cultivated with plastic Dixie tumblers of Dewar's, and for whom he'd forgiven months of back rent in exchange for a promised rendezvous with his wife.

"She's all yours soon as I leave the house on Saturday," Chris elbowed him Friday night up in the garage apartment, as he spilled lines of meth onto the glass coffee table he'd moved up from the patio. "She's ready for you all right, you'll see. And if you finish her, the house is yours." They each snorted a few lines. Jim rubbed some on his gums and behind his ears, which Chris thought troubling, but didn't create enough data in his brain to draw a conclusion.

Now, as he listens to an all-news radio station, Chris focuses on the fantasy—an adobe house with a backyard brick oven, a smoke pit, and a small still, if he can figure out how to make his own mescal. The reverie breaks as he spots a dim pulsing red light looming in the rear-view mirror, practically bleeding through the rear cab window. As he nudges the truck's wheels onto the interstate's gravel-spitting shoulder, a state trooper skids in behind.

Tina has on the new Beats Chris bought her as a road trip gift, which is why she doesn't hear the more distant sirens, the gaggle of sound swelling behind them. Tina also can't hear the radio newscaster, who at that moment announces that Chris is the prime person of interest in the Connecticut murder of a heroic Gulf War veteran, a Purple Heart award-winner, named Jim Berger.

Otherwise, she would have started screaming "kidnapper" and "freakin' pedophile" and "dog fucker" right then in the truck, before the officers approached. It would have saved her the humiliation of having to do so in front of the mob of press cameras outside the Cockeysville, Maryland town square as the journalists jockeyed for glimpses of Chris, handcuffed wrists hidden under a blazer, as he was led up the courthouse steps.

About the author:

John Francis Istel has worked as an actor, parked cars as a valet, taught as an adjunct at Medgar Evers College and at NYU (where he received an MFA), bartended in Times Square, and raised a family in Brooklyn, where he curates Word Cabaret, a reading series. His poetry and fiction have appeared in *Belmont Story Review*, *New Letters*, *Weave*, *WordRiot*, *Linden Avenue*, *Rappahannock Review*, *Up the Staircase* (Pushcart Prize nominee), *Soundings Review* and many others. Before becoming a NYC public high school teacher, he worked as a magazine/book editor and wrote about theater for Atlantic, Elle, The Village Voice, and elsewhere. Recently, he completed a short fiction collection, *Internal Bleeding and Other Love Stories*.

EUPHORIA, VA
©2019 by Katelyn Andell

Elizabeth Taylor once visited our town back in the seventies. In their retelling, the older ladies throw back their heads and clap their elegantly manicured hands in laughter with the control of playing scales on a trumpet. It seems to be the trademark of that generation, as if their mothers had absorbed the essence of Scarlett O'Hara from the silver screen and pumped it through their umbilical cords.

Taylor was married to Senator John Warner when she made her legendary visit. He was her sixth husband, and I'm sure by then she was used to being paraded around like some kind of circus lion, although rarely in an actual parade—much less during a festival honoring the unglamorous peanut. "I'm so happy to be here in Euphoria," she told the locals, not only botching the name of the town but ascribing to it a feeling so out of reach for most people. At the end of the story, the ladies' laughter dissolves and they are left looking out the window, realizing that the town's glory days have long since passed.

The town, in its heyday, must have been a bustling hub of agriculture. Faded paint on the sides of the grand brick buildings on Main Street advertise the Hotel Virginia and defunct brands of soda and tobacco. Now, the store fronts are either empty or house pawn shops, gambling ventures, or law offices. New restaurants pop up now and then, and for a moment you think that the town is experiencing a renaissance. But they are open for a couple of years at best before shuttering their doors in defeat.

I grew up here, went to school here, had my first kiss here, but no matter how thick my drawl was, I was still an outsider. Unlike my friends, my family came from elsewhere—New York, Florida, Arizona, Iowa. I had no grandparents in town to visit on Friday afternoons and no cousins nearby that I could wrap my arms around and proclaim my "kin." Adults would ask me who my parents are and after telling them, they'd squint their eyes as if reaching into the family trees for some connection.

I liked it this way, being an outsider. "You can go anywhere, do anything," my parents told me. "There's nothing keeping you here." They pictured me becoming a doctor, a lawyer, maybe a diplomat—some title that carried prestige. The more they wanted it for me, the more I wanted it for myself, and their dreams became mine and I let them float me high above the heads of my peers and the crumbling buildings and the pickup trucks. Although I was quiet and somewhat likable, there were still those girls who looked me up and down and wondered who the hell I thought I was.

Who I was, was not this town. I concealed my low opinion of the place as best as I could until I packed up and left for college. Being around city kids and wealthy suburbanites had a surprising effect on me. During introductory chatter, I described where I was from in colorful, exaggerated anecdotes to elicit giggles and raised eyebrows. In doing so, the town became a permanent part of my identity as a nickname, a punchline. I lost my drawl but it doesn't matter—I am Euphoria and Euphoria is me.

When I go home for Christmas next week, I won't stay long. I'm afraid of the effect nostalgia might play if I get too comfortable. I have a good job in D.C. as a congressional staffer, which consumes about ten hours of my day. After work I sip cocktails in a bar with exposed brick and old-fashioned light bulbs before returning to my apartment on H Street. I trade my heels for kitty cat slippers and watch an episode of whatever crime show is popular at the moment. The next day I repeat the process, only instead of cocktails I meet friends for pho or ramen. Tonight's meal is vegan fried chicken over waffles.

"Incredible. Almost tastes like the real thing," I say with my mouth full of textured soy.

"I bet you could serve that to your neighbors back home and they'd never know the difference."

"Maybe. But the arugula garnish would make them suspicious."

Everyone laughs when I say things like this because it confirms their belief that red meat America is holding the country back. They came to D.C. from other major cities to save America from the inside, and I am one of them, playing the role of a spy who crosses enemy lines during the holidays.

"Once the rednecks get a taste of single-payer healthcare and vegan fried chicken, they'll never go back." I say. We all laugh. I take a sip of my gin and tonic to wash away the guilt.

I pack a suitcase with four days' worth of clothes and presents for Mom and Dad before descending into the parking garage. My Volkswagen still has that new car smell even though it is three years old. I follow the signs to I-95 and get stuck in holiday traffic for hours, but luckily, I've downloaded enough true crime podcasts on my iPhone to last to Miami and back. Traffic is much lighter south of Fredericksburg, and once I pass Richmond, each mile marker offers less and less. I stop for gas and grab a coffee at the last Starbucks on the interstate until North Carolina.

I arrive at seven in the evening and already the roads are empty. Big lighted snowflakes illuminate Main Street, reminding me of something Dad says every Christmas when they decorate the downtown: "They do what they can." Of course, *they* doesn't include him, although he's lived here for thirty years now. I park on the street in front of our house, a brick colonial into which my parents have poured thousands of dollars of their teacher salaries. It looks nicer than when I lived in it: there's a new roof, new eco-friendly windows, and a fancy kitchen with those drawers that shut themselves. A house like this would easily cost half a million in the Washington suburbs, but it will be hard to sell down here. I open the front door to the smell of a balsam scented candle and the sound of Nat King Cole crooning in the kitchen. The Christmas tree is decorated in multi-colored mini bulbs and covered with quirky ornaments. Suddenly, I forget my age.

"Amy!" Dad's voice bellows. He's coming out of the bathroom still zipping up his jeans. He's still pretty thin, though a belly is quietly spilling over his pants. He looks older, grayer. I run over to hug him.

"How're things in the People's House?" he asks.

"That's the White House, Dad," I smile. "Same old stuff...you know, idealism, obstruction, lost causes. Corruption. Rinse and repeat."

He pats me on the back. "You'll fix it."

The music is so loud that Mom doesn't hear me come into the kitchen at first. She hands me an overfull glass of wine without asking if I want any.

"Merry Christmas, Mom," I tell her after putting down the glass. She kisses me on the cheek and asks if my drive was okay, and if I've seen that senator we both hate lurking around my apartment building lately. She's making a stir fry—she's self-conscious of her cooking, as I've taken her to "foodie" restaurants in D.C. with exotic ingredients she can't find at Food Lion. The stir fry is simple, and sounds exotic.

I notice that the cat's food bowl is missing and wonder where she is. I perform a cursory search for Punk in all of her usual haunts: under the hutch, behind the piano, resting on the pillows of my twin-sized bed.

"Have you seen Punk around?" I ask Mom. Mom stops stirring.

"Shit," she whispers. My heart stops.

"Mom? What happened to Punk?"

I'm told that Punk escaped from the house last week. She has spent her nineteen years inside, knowing nothing about the outside world except what she could see from the porch. There was enough hunting to do inside that kept her busy—we thought.

"Didn't you even try to look for her?" My voice is loud and shaky. Dad comes in.

"We tried, honey," he said. "But you know, when older cats run away, they don't want to be found."

I don't drink the wine. Instead, I grab my coat and drive to the sports bar on the outskirts of town, next to the truck stop. I go inside and head straight for the bartender. I can feel eyes on me and wonder if anyone recognizes me. The bartender is pudgy with a floppy haircut framing a round face. He's wearing a tee shirt with an eagle flying majestically across a waving American flag, the kind of shirt that my friends in Washington would wear ironically. He's familiar, but I can't place him. He tilts his head toward me as he cleans a glass. A smile of self-satisfaction spreads across his face when he finally remembers who I am.

"Amy," he says. "Haven't seen you in years. How the hell are you?"

"Okay. Live in D.C. now. Home for Christmas."

He nods. "I know, I've seen your posts on Facebook. You eat out a lot, don't you?"

"It's what you do there."

"Hey, I'm not judging. If I lived there and had the cash, I would eat good too."

Despite being Facebook friends, I still don't know who he is; worse, I don't think I should ask him. I order a gin and tonic and he delivers before moving on to other customers. I try to focus on a basketball game that's playing on one of the screens above me, but I'm not all that interested in sports. My mind keeps wandering back to Punk: her little face with the white spot just above her nose, her tail that she liked to whip around when annoyed, how she would purr into my pillow when I slept. I feel the tears flooding to the front of my eyes and I knock my head back so gravity can do its work.

The bartender comes back around. "You okay?"

"No. My cat ran away."

"Oh shit, I'm sorry."

"I was eleven when we got her."

"That really sucks." He gives me a refill on the house.

"Why is it that in movies, the death of a beloved pet is overshadowed by all of the other shit going on?"

He looks confused, so I elaborate. "You know, in horror movies they always kill the dog first, because they know what's going on. They have that sixth sense. But the family barely blinks because they're about to die themselves, and at the end of the movie when everything's okay, nothing is said about the dog who was trying to protect them from evil in the first place."

"Oh, yeah, I guess, but those are extreme circumstances, right? What about *Marley & Me?* That whole movie was about the dog. Or *Hachi*? Damn, if you haven't seen that one, you should probably forget I said anything because that shit is *sad*. I'm a dude and I don't mind admitting that I was sobbing watching that dog wait for his master at that train station."

"Okay, that's true, but—"

"Or what about those old classics? We watched *Where the Red Fern Grows* in school and I'm telling you, all the boys were crying."

"No tragic cat deaths, though."

The bartender thinks about this. Neither one of us can come up with a single movie with a tragic cat death.

I crack a smile, but it's short-lived. "All I'm saying is, I'm a thirty-year-old woman crying over my dead cat when other people my age have really important stuff to think about. I mean, most girls I graduated with are divorced with kids. A couple of guys died in car accidents. One guy—remember Chris Jeffries?—killed himself in his living room. And here I am, drinking because of a cat. But she was *important* to me, you know? She was a friend."

There are two older women sitting next to me and I can tell that they are eavesdropping. Our eyes meet for a moment, and the one with the dark edge-of-night roots peeking through her blonde hair touches my arm.

"Sorry for your loss," she says. "Pets are members of the family."

"Yeah, we love them just the same," the other woman rejoins. She's wearing pajama pants with Christmas trees on them.

"Thanks."

I check my watch: it's almost ten. I'm exhausted and embarrassed about running out of the house like an angsty teenager. I consider driving home, but the drinks were strong and I haven't eaten dinner.

"Wait," the bartender declares. "Didn't you say your cat ran away? You don't know for sure that she's dead, do you?"

"Well, no. But she's old and she's been gone a week. Cats like to go off and die in peace."

"But there's a chance she's not dead," he whispers, as if this is an epiphany.

The pajama pant lady's eyes widen. "You know, sometimes cats will wander off out of their neighborhood and nice folks take 'em in. She could be sittin' warm and comfy under a Christmas tree." The other woman nods enthusiastically.

The bartender leans on the counter and looks sincerely into my eyes. It makes me a little uncomfortable. "I want to help you find your cat."

We make a plan: I'm going to send a photo to Donna, the woman with edge-of-night hair, and she will post it on the community Facebook page. Pajama Pants, whose name is Stephanie, is going to post signs on telephone poles around town. The bartender is going to come over in the morning and we are going to plant cans of tuna everywhere within a three-mile radius. I hear Donna call him Chase, and I repeat his name several times at the end of the night to prove I knew it all along.

The next day is Christmas Eve, but no one minds. Finding my cat would be some kind of Christmas miracle, they declare, befitting a Hallmark movie.

Mom and Dad have left the front door unlocked for me. I'm thankful but irritated at the same time because it's completely unsafe. I remind myself not to lecture them about it and tiptoe up the stairs to my twin bed so I don't wake them. I strip down to just my underwear because I've left my suitcase downstairs and I don't feel like getting it. The spot on my pillow where Punk usually sleeps feels warm, but maybe it's just the alcohol messing with my head.

Light floods through my bedroom windows the next morning. I check the time: Chase will be here soon. I throw on some jeans and my college sweatshirt and make my way downstairs, where both parents are standing in the kitchen with cups of coffee.

"Morning, Amy," Dad begins as he steps towards me. "Listen..."

"I'm sorry if I overreacted," I mumble. I'm groggy and hungover and the words come out slowly. "I didn't get to say goodbye, and I feel like I owe it to her to at least try to find her. If she's dead, I'll bury her. But I need to try."

Dad frowns. "Do you want some help?"

Mom rolls her eyes, but doesn't say anything.

"No, I have some already. Some people from the Corner Pocket offered to help last night." I can tell that Dad wants to protest. "I'm a thirty-year-old woman, and they are nice people. I'll be fine. I'll be home by five at the latest."

Dad nods because he knows he won't be able to stop me and understands that he shouldn't try. He wishes me luck.

Chase's truck is bright blue with boxy edges and a toolbox in the bed. It's old—he probably bought it cheap to fix up. I can hear his loud exhaust from two streets away and when he pulls up, his engine is vibrating. Country music is playing on the radio and suddenly I'm transported to my high school days. In private, I derided their trucks and their hunting rifles and the politics they inherited from their parents, but I never turned down rides to the mall or free meals from Wendy's. I'm already thinking of how I will tell my friends about my redneck Christmas Eve. The blast of the exhaust snaps me out of it and reminds me why his truck is parked in front of my house in the first place.

"You get the tuna?" he asks, pronouncing it "toe-na."

"Damn. No, I forgot. I just woke up."

"You drank a lot last night, that's probably part of it," he chuckles.

"Yeah. I'll just run inside and grab it."

I feel thankful that Mom and Dad aren't in the kitchen when I go back in. I pack a Wal-Mart bag full of StarKist and I'm back outside in less than a minute. Chase is talking on his phone to Stephanie, who reports that Phase One is complete: Donna has posted the picture of Punk on Facebook and already ten people have shared it. Phase Two has run into a problem, though. Stephanie's printer has run out of ink, so she's going to see if Wal-Mart will print them off since the library is closed on Christmas Eve.

"You could just buy the ink at Wal-Mart," he suggests with slight irritation. He hangs up and we set off, starting first in the backyard. It slopes down to a creek but is mostly devoid of foliage and places for old cats to hide. We walk silently until Chase starts calling, "Punk! Here, kitty!"

"Here, kitty-kitty-kitty-kitty!" I echo in percussive bursts. We follow the curves of the creek flowing alongside the river named for the Native American tribe that used to hunt along its banks. This part of the river is brown and foamy thanks to the churn from the dam. When I was a kid, it reminded me of root beer.

"There's a lot of glass back here," Chase mutters as he looks down. "Did you play back here as a kid? Seems dangerous."

"Yeah, funny thing: this used to be a dump way back in the day," I say. "Like, in the early nineteen-hundreds."

"And the person who built your house saw the pile of crap and said, 'Hey, this would make a great view!'"

"I bet the lot was cheap, though." We both laugh. The ground beneath us is rich and fertile and, if one digs a foot or so in the soil, glittering with old glass. Over the years, Dad has found several unchipped medicine bottles from one hundred years ago—the kind on which an antiques enthusiast might spend twenty bucks for the essential purpose of holding ten Q-tips or a sprig of lavender in her bathroom.

As I look at the ground, I notice Chase's boots. They are heavy-duty and stiff, covered in camouflage and dried mud. In high school, the guys would make cuts in their jeans so that they would fit over their "clodhoppers," as Mom called them.

"Do you hunt?" I ask, but I know the answer. Why else would he have camouflage boots?

"Yeah, mostly deer. Maybe you saw it on Facebook—I shot a really nice buck back a month or two ago."

"No, I missed that. You getting him mounted?" I'm trying to use what I think is a hunter's lingo, but it feels clumsy. In truth, the thought of shooting a deer makes me sick to my stomach.

"Yep. For my living room. He'll be my third."

We take a few steps in silence. The bubbling of the creek seems loud all of a sudden; then, as if it is a sign, he pulls back the lid of a can of tuna and lays it on the ground.

"Don't you think it's funny," I begin, "that you kill animals for fun and yet here you are, helping me find my cat?"

"No," he answers. He seems unbothered by my judgmental tone. "Cats aren't the same as deer. They're pets. People don't keep deer as pets. Hunting deer is a part of the country culture. It's more about the time in the woods than about the animal. Plus, there are just too many of 'em. I see deer killed on the side of the road all the time. They'll kill a driver in a heartbeat."

"A lot of people say there are too many cats. They're invasive species, actually. They kill a lot of birds."

Unconvinced, Chase shakes his head. "If you shoot cats, you're a psychopath. You can't go around shooting a little girl's pet." His smile is sincere, and I feel myself blush despite his boots and enthusiasm for hunting. We follow the creek to the end of the neighborhood that leads into thick brush and woods. The leaves crunch underneath my feet and their dampness brushes against the patch of skin between my pants cuffs and ankle socks.

Behind me, I hear a faint rustling. I'm sure that it's Punk trotting along to the call of her name, but it's one of thousands of squirrels that scurry around our peripheries, unloved and unnoticed. Chase bends down and opens another can of tuna.

"Squirrels don't eat tuna, do they?" he asks.

"Don't think so. But I bet possums would."

"Call it a Christmas present, then."

We continue to walk along, investigating every dark shadow and hollow tree. Besides the rotting wood, I'm surprised by the lack of dead things I see. I wonder where all the animals go to die, and whether there is some gathering spot that the animals have chosen. Perhaps they have a pet cemetery of their own. Chase likes the idea; we imagine animals both wild and domesticated converging to participate in the circle of life.

"Can I ask you kind of a personal question?" Chase says.

"Of course."

"What made you leave town? Like, what is so great about living in a big city?"

I measure my words carefully. "Well, there are more jobs there, for one thing. What I wanted to do—federal policymaking—I can't do here. There's also more to do, with all the concerts and museums and festivals. And, there's more diversity." Every time I mention something I love about the city, I worry that I am putting him down, like it's a zero-sum game. One point scored for the city life means a loss for Euphoria.

"We have lots of black people here, though."

"I'm not talking about just black and white. I'm talking about people from all over the world. There's more than just racial diversity, too—there's different religions, different ideas, different economic classes."

"So, you're saying it's more interesting there. I guess I understand that. But don't you miss the trees, and the space, and the quiet?"

I nod. "Sure, sometimes. I come back a few times a year, and usually a few days is all I need. Then I'm ready for the noise of the city. It has a way of drowning out all of the unpleasant thoughts in my head."

Chase grunts and stops walking. He kicks at the ground with his boot. "That's just not me, I guess. You know, I did pretty well in school. I wasn't valedictorian or anything, but I made honor roll. My whole family's here. I like it that way, being able to eat dinner with them on Thursdays and Sundays, knowing that if they need me, I'm just a few miles down the road. I like that I can buy a house at a decent price with a bunch of trees so I can't see my neighbor. I like that if I need anything, I can call on my neighbor, even though we are half a mile apart. I like the idea that whoever I marry, I probably already know the girl, because we went to the same elementary school. I like that the world seems far away."

"But this *is* the world. You can't pretend like you're not part of it, like your actions exist in a vacuum."

"I never said that I'm not part of it."

"But you want the world to pay for your lifestyle, don't you? Do you know how much fossil fuels your truck burns into our atmosphere? Do you realize how many gun deaths there are in this country? But you don't want any restrictions on guns because 'blah-blah-Second Amendment-don't-tread-on-me. "

"Hold on. What are we even talking about?"

"I'm talking about the ignorance of your lifestyle."

Chase makes a face like I've punched him in the gut. He shakes his head. "That's not fair. You think you know me, but you don't."

"You're right, I'm sorry."

"You only asked me one single question about myself, today and yesterday, and it was about hunting. I guess that's all I'm about, right? I'm just a redneck simpleton to you."

Tears start forming in my eyes but I don't want him to see it, so I kick at the ground too. A childish "sorry" is all I can manage before I start walking ahead and calling out Punk's name.

Two hours pass and we don't speak much. The search becomes

more half-hearted as it slowly dawns on me that Punk is, in all likelihood, dead. She didn't want us to find her lifeless body behind the couch or even behind a tree in the backyard—she wanted to spare us. Those who are scientific-minded might sigh heavily and explain that love is just a chemical reaction in our brains rather than a function of the mythological soul. Then they would point out that animals act out of instinct rather than out of consideration for humans.

Chase is not one of these people. I turn around and cry into his flannel shirt and he hugs me with a kind of country-boy chivalry that is not awkward at all, despite my rudeness earlier.

"She's in kitty heaven," he says gently. "All the tuna she can eat, lots of mice to hunt, and laser pointers everywhere. Y'all gave her a good life."

When I'm finished crying, we turn around and walk back toward my house. Stephanie calls and says she's posted ten flyers but needs to go home and start cooking for Christmas. Chase turns away from the phone in my direction and asks if we should tell her not to bother with the flyers. I shake my head, because you just never know.

About the author:

Katelyn Andell has called many places home, from rural Virginia to the Black Forest in Germany. As a middle school special educator, she encourages her students to be creative whenever possible. She finds joy in reading and writing historical fiction, complex family sagas, and twisted psychological thrillers. Euphoria, VA is her first published work of fiction, although she has been writing since she could hold a pencil. Katelyn has one completed novel entitled *Photographs from Saint-Lô* and hopes to see it in print one day. She lives in Wake Forest, North Carolina with her husband, dog, and cat.

NEVER IN GRACE
©2019 by Carol Cooley

Father Daniel stood outside the ornate wooden doors trying to steady his mouth in the frigid air. My fingers were moist from their dip into holy water as I pulled on Mother's forearm to rush us past him and straight to the car. It was one of the coldest winter days growing up that I can remember. A bitter day of fateful choices.

Mother stopped. "Let's just say a quick hello," she said.

I rolled my eyes and hoped she wouldn't launch into another story about how they grew up in the same parish. Seconds later he was facing us. He cupped her hand and winked at me.

"Lydia, how are you?" he said to Mother.

Father Daniel seemed more nervous than cold. His eyes were squinty and his grin was locked in place. There was something oily about him, even in brutal, dry weather.

"Good, good, good," Mother said.

"Well, that is terrific," he said.

Irritated by her obedience, my grip on her arm tightened as their hands rhythmically moved up and down until Father Daniel let go and moved onto pleasantries with other people. Mother and I darted to the far corner of the parking lot. Our boots splashed the salty slush onto our lower legs and by the time we reached the car her pantyhose was thoroughly speckled. She dug for the keys while I tried to tuck both hands into my coat sleeves.

"I think I know why pews are so hard," I said.

Her eyes were focused in her purse. "Why is that, Hanna?" she asked.

"Because Mass is so boring. If they were padded, we'd fall asleep within fifteen minutes."

I felt proud of my comment—the way young teenagers do when they think they had a clever thought. Mother walked towards the front of the car until she could see me. The look in her eyes forced me into stillness. Like a bull pawing at the earth, steam flowed from her nostrils as my legs trembled for reasons other than the winter air.

"Why would you say something so disrespectful?" she demanded.

There were globs of mascara on her eyelashes and the daylight exposed an uneven layer of taupe foundation. Although her imperfections were soothing, I stuttered my next words.

"I—I thought that it would be...."

She did not let me finish and the sting on my face lingered like the sound of a cymbal. She turned her back to me, walked to the driver's side, and stayed in the car several seconds before opening my lock. On the ride home, I willed her to look back at me, but she never did. Her eyes seemed to bounce around, like they were attached to puppet strings in the back of her head. I signed my name on the fogged-up window until I ran out of space. *Hanna Brennan, Hanna Brennan, Hanna Brennan.*

Mother tensed up when we reached our snow-covered driveway. She shot barbs at Dad every winter about his no-shovel standard. Dad was from the South and even after living in western Pennsylvania for twenty years he still defended that clearing snow was the sun's job. The car crunched the ice as Mother kept the tires in the tracks. She could be so precise when she wanted. With one final pump, we were inside the garage. Dad's car, a baby blue Pontiac Bonneville, sat in his spot—clean, dry, and barely used since his lay-off from the mill a year prior. I kicked off a clump of dirty snow clinging to our back bumper.

"Don't do that," Mother snapped. "You'll make a mess in here."

"I could tell Father Daniel that you hit me," I blurted as if I was threatening to tell on a sibling.

Mother stopped, but didn't turn around. She finally went up the steps and let the door close as I stood in place, listening to drips of thawing ice.

Inside, Dad's bald head was poking out of the headrest and the room had a light haze of smoke. "All in the Family" was on and there was a bowl on the side table with potato chip crumbs. Our home was a classic seventies split-level with rust shag carpet and fake wood paneling. Dad spent all day in his tweed recliner tapping ashes from his Salem into a three-tiered ashtray stand. He woke up for two meals a day, poured a martini no earlier than four-thirty, and went to bed by nine. His God was the Pittsburgh Pirates baseball team and he never uttered a negative word unless you asked him a question during a game. I sat on the couch across from him.

"Hey, Dad," I said.

"Well, hey there. How was church-mass?"

"Just Mass, Dad." I giggled and looked around for mother. "It was boring."

"Boring? Well, that's probably because you're not saying the right prayers."

I took off my coat. "Okay. What kind of prayer should I be saying?"

Dad stood up in the same Wrangler jeans he wore every weekend since I'd been alive. The fabric between his legs was faded and his black and red flannel shirt was neatly tucked in. An aged leather belt wrapped around his trim waist.

"So, the first thing you do is salute properly," he said. He put his right hand up to his forehead. "Like this. And it can't be limp or halfhearted."

I covered my smile.

"No, no, don't laugh," he said. "A salute is the ultimate form of respect." Dad wasn't a veteran. "Then you take a deep breath and look the thing straight in the eye."

"And what thing is that?" I asked.

"What thing? Come on, you know what thing." He rolled his eyes. "From there, you say what's in your heart. I mean really in your heart. That's what God wants."

"I'm ready," I said.

"Okay, here goes. Our Father who art in heaven with Roberto Clemente who was the greatest baseball player to ever live. Hallowed be thy first game of the season. Thy kingdom of the Pirates come. Thy World Series be won. On the mound which is built like a little slice of heaven. Amen."

I was in a full cackle when mother walked into the room. She stared us down like a guard with her eye on the bad ones and went into the kitchen. Dad shrugged his shoulders and sat back down in his chair. A second later he was reaching for a cigarette and staring at the TV. I went over and leaned into his ear.

"That prayer was funny," I whispered.

He forced a smile and it made me want to tell him about Mother smacking me. Instead, I stood up and announced, "I'm not doing Confirmation!"

Dad's eyes grew big and round and the sound of mother stacking dishes got louder. Neither of them said what they were thinking, so I went upstairs to my room.

After that day, Mother walked into my room on Sunday at nine-thirty in the morning and said it was time to go to Mass. Each time I shook my head. On the sixth Sunday, she didn't ask. Instead, she took a handful of albums from the rack, pulled my favorite shirt off its hanger, and slapped a Bible down on the dresser. I was sitting on my bed reading *Teen* magazine and chewing bubble gum like the end was near.

"You can only control me for so long," I said as she was leaving.

She turned back around. "Mother's control their daughters forever, Hanna. You'll see that someday."

I walked over to the dresser and picked up the Bible. I thought about using it for some travel plans like when kids spin a globe, stop it with pointed finger, and say, "Here's where I'm going to live."

I opened it and landed on Sirach Chapter Four—The Rewards of Wisdom.

Wisdom instructs her children and admonishes those who seek her. He who loves her loves life; those who seek her out win her favor.

The word "wisdom" and the pronoun "she" left me with a peaceful feeling—a reprieve from "Father" and "He" and watching all the nuns live in subservience. My thoughts were soon distracted by Mother's voice. I cracked open my door and heard her pleading with Dad to get me back into Church and her path for me. She was desperate to acknowledge my bond with Dad.

"James. Please talk to her," she said. "Hanna cannot skip this part of her faith."

My image of Dad was clear. He was in the recliner, staring at the TV, half hearing her, and feeling impatient because she wasn't leaving at her regular time.

"James!" she screamed. "Look at me!"

"Lydia, Hanna is going to do what she wants. She's growing up. Let her find her way."

My heart was slamming into my breastbone.

"You're a passionless excuse for a man," she said.

I cupped my hand over my mouth. A minute later, Mother left. I looked back down at the Bible and ripped the page clean out. I pulled the warm pink wad from my mouth, stuck it on the word *wisdom*, and turned it into a paper ball. A second later it was laid to rest at the bottom of the garbage can.

After that day, things went back to being as routine as a monk's Tuesday. I went to school and spent Friday nights at the skating rink. The bend towards spring was in sight and I craved the bare ground so I could run and drill all the confusion and disconnection straight into the earth. But just as I was getting comfortable in my religious boycott, Mother was loosening her big guns from the rack. It was a Saturday and I had just shoved a fork-full of pancakes in my mouth when she told me that Father Daniel would be coming to the house to help me "work through my problem." *The Exorcist* was in the theatres and the week before I saw Mother choke a dishtowel while watching the preview on television.

"Please don't do this," I begged her. "I'm not that girl from the movie."

"Hanna, I've had enough. You will stay in the Church. Whatever it takes."

I set my fork down and stared at her. She was hugging her waist. Her navy turtleneck clung to her, and a crucifix dangled from a long chain and rested between her breasts. All the kitchen cabinets were open and the dishwasher was ready to be emptied. She pulled out glasses and stacked them in a row. Her hair was coming undone in the back from bobby pins popping out of their secure spaces.

"When is he coming?" I asked.

"Any minute," she said, "and you will not embarrass me."

"Today!" I screamed.

From dishwasher to cabinet, her platform shoes drummed the linoleum as my abandoned pancakes absorbed all the syrup and turned cold. I stood up, pushed my chair in, and took my plate to the sink.

"What about your breakfast?"

"I'm done," I said. "Fresh syrup can't bring these back to life."

"Where are you going?" she asked.

"My room."

My bedroom walls were bright orange. I owed Dad for that. He worked hard to convince Mother to let me have that color, but it was coming back to him that day. The concern in her voice felt like a vapor searching for an open window.

"Why did those damn walls have to be painted orange?" I heard her say.

"What do you mean?" Dad asked.

"Father Daniel is coming over to talk with Hanna. If she doesn't come down, he'll have to go upstairs."

A stretch of silence followed. I imagined Dad looking hypnotized and waiting for someone to snap their fingers.

"Father Daniel is coming here? Why didn't you tell me sooner?"

"Yes, here," Mother said. "He's coming to help change her mind about Catechism. What will he think of those walls?"

"The walls?" Dad asked. "He's a man of faith, Lydia, he's supposed to be unassuming, right?"

His voice was shaky and I started to wonder if he was afraid of Father Daniel.

"Right," she said. "He shouldn't care."

"Should we get some food out? Maybe cheese and crackers?" Dad said.

"Good!" Mother said. "Yes, cheese and crackers."

I felt nauseous with the image of them ripping apart Kraft cheese slices and sticking them on Triscuits. I slammed the door shut and quickly tried to imagine Father Daniel in my room. Books were scattered from headrest to footboard; *The Outsiders, The Pigman, Go Ask Alice.* I looked in the mirror. "Jeans again?" Mother would say. There I stood in bell-bottomed Levi's, a red poncho hiding breast buds, and long wavy hair with the tips still golden from a summer's dose of chlorine. I picked up the Bible from the dresser and went to hide it under the bed when I heard Father Daniel and Mother talking as they walked up the stairs. I quickly sat down. Without knocking, she opened the door and let him in.

"Father Daniel, don't mind the color in here. Children make these kinds of choices without thinking. Please have a fruitful visit," she said before closing the door.

Father Daniel cupped his hands and sat down next to me on the bed. I had never been that close to him. His nose was pointy and coarse black hair poked through the cheeks surface. Tiny purple lines were all over his face like unnamed rivers on a map. I smelled something that would sting if it hit your eyes. Cologne maybe.

"Hanna, you're reading the Bible. That's good."

I pinched my lips shut and wanted to toss it on his lap like a hot potato. I set it down and gripped my hands between my thighs. Father Daniel put his hand on my knee and gave it a light squeeze.

"You know why I'm here, don't you?" he asked.

"Sort of," I said.

He sighed and closed his eyes. "Hanna, I'm here because your mother says you don't want to do Confirmation. Is that true?"

He raised his right eyebrow as I wiggled my knee to get him to release it. I hid my hands under my poncho. His voice grew stern as he folded his arms.

"Why not?" he asked.

"I'd rather read and study on Sundays," I said. I really didn't know the answer.

Father Daniel stood up and carefully circled my room, looking at everything like he was studying artifacts at the museum. He sat back down in the same spot.

"Confirmation is about accepting responsibility for your faith and belief system," he said.

I nodded.

He exhaled with pursed lips. "Hanna, you're old enough where I can be straight with you. Can I be straight with you?"

I nodded again.

"Leaving the Church now could make for a horrifying future," he said.

The skin on his face looked like it was tightening to its limits from wide eyes and flared nostrils. He rubbed his hands together like he was trying to ignite fire from two sticks. "It's cold in here," he said and paused for several seconds. "Where was I?"

"You were about to tell me something about the future," I said.

"Right. Girls, rather young ladies, who don't finish Catechism can end up in horrifying situations. You see, because they don't know the Church or Jesus, they end up choosing things that they think make them feel better. Scary things. Do you understand?"

"Not really," I said.

He hung his head down. "Hanna, I'm just going to say it—they do things whores would do. They might become prostitutes, or worse."

Feeling his gaze on me, I stared straight ahead and searched for something to say during the quiet between us. "What could be worse than that?" I finally asked.

"Well. I guess a prostitute on drugs," he said. "Or one who takes off her clothes dancing to Disco."

My eyes were shifting side to side. When I finally looked at him, I was as horrified as any prostitute on drugs stripping to Disco. He was grinning and shaking his head up and down. My body stiffened.

"I'm pretty sure that won't happen to me," I said.

"Oh, Hanna, you're naïve. There are horrifying things out there."

Every time he said "horrifying" he emphasized "horr", and I started to wonder if he just liked saying that word. Father Daniel stooped down in front of me and put his hand above my knee again.

"We are going to talk more about this next week," he said.

For several minutes I listened to Father Daniel and Mother's muffled voices downstairs until the front door opened. I went to the window and watched him walk down the steps to his orange AMC Pacer parked on the street. A minute later, Mother charged up the stairs. I ran back to the bed just as the door flew open.

"Well?" she said, catching her breath. "How'd it go? Father Daniel said you're very special and he wants to come back next week."

I didn't respond. Mother moved around the room with the energy of a songbird at the first sign of spring. She mumbled to herself how blessed she was that a priest would take his time to come to the house. A few minutes later, Dad was in my room, too.

"Sweetie," he said. "How'd it go?"

As soon as our eyes met, a cry from deep within poured out. I covered my face with my hands, bent over, and sobbed in my lap. He sat down next to me and rested his hand on my back.

"Wait, honey, why are you crying?"

I looked up at Mother's flat expression. Her arms were around her waist and she squinted at me. I turned to Dad.

"Please don't let Father Daniel come back here."

"Why not?" Dad asked.

"He's creepy," I said. I tried to find a solid inhale.

"What do mean by creepy?" He looked at Mother, then me, then back at her.

I couldn't say anymore and asked that they both leave. Mother told me mid-week that Father Daniel was coming again, and he came every weekend for almost two months. Each visit he would put his hand on my knee and tell a story about sacrifice and loyalty to the Church. They started with other people's stories – how his grandparents were immigrants and left their families in Europe for something better and how his sister Jean sacrificed her kidney for his Aunt Betty. On the last day I saw him, he told me two more stories of sacrifice—his and Christ's.

The roads were mostly just wet from melting curb-side snow and there were patches of green grass finally visible in yards. Father Daniel was different that day. His black hair was slicked back with something firm. He made quick turns with his head and body, not like the calculated movements I was used to. I was sitting on the bed in my usual position—hands under something, feet tapping the floor, and wanting to be somewhere else. *Anywhere* else. After Mother shut the door, Father Daniel hurried in front of me and stooped down. He made a strange arch with his brows larger than I thought would be humanly possible and he had a broad smile that looked like a set of charged ivory piano keys.

"Hanna," he said, "I'm very excited to see you today. Do you know why?"

I shook my head.

"I think we can move past all this today." He took out a metal cross the size of my hand with Jesus attached to the front. "Hold this," he said.

He placed the cross in my palm then guided my fingers around it.

"Did you know that Jesus sacrificed for you? He gave up all of his power as God to become like us so he could give us eternal life. Do you understand the intensity of this sacrifice?"

"I think so," I said, "but is it really a sacrifice if it's something he wanted to do?"

Father Daniel pushed more firmly on my hand, forcing me to hold it tighter. He got on both knees, put his face inches from mine, and said, "Screw your questions." He crushed my hand into the cross harder until the sharp points cut into my fingers. I tried to cry and release from the pressure, but he stayed firm and stared at me with an eerie satisfaction.

In a whimper I said, "That hurts, Father."

He kept squeezing. "Well, this is what it's all about, Hanna. Pain and sacrifice. Do you think I really wanted to become a priest? Do you think I wanted to spend my time helping whores, or that it was easy for me to give up college and cars and women? No, it wasn't. I sacrificed. Sacrifice is surrendering to what's worth more than yourself and sometimes that is painful."

He finally let go of my hand and the cross fell to the floor. Two of my fingers were bleeding. I started to shiver as I rubbed out the dents in my skin. Father Daniel stood above me and tried to run his hands through his stiff hair.

"Anything, Hanna? Anything?" he said.

I swallowed. "You're upset because you became a priest?"

He charged towards me with a backhand then stopped. He smiled at my flinch and gently ran the back of his hand down the side of my face.

"Life isn't going to work out for you, Hanna," he said. "You can't do anything without God, the Church, and sacrifice."

He said he wouldn't be coming back and left. On his way outside, I heard him tell Mother that I wasn't capable of being in the Church and to keep praying for me. From my window, I watched him walk out to his car for the last time then went to the stereo and blasted Sly and the Family Stone's *It's a Family Affair*.

Mother barged in and pulled the needle off the record.

"Well, you win, Hanna. I hope you're happy."

I was crying and asked her to come to me. She shook her head and left. I grabbed the Bible from under the bed, and cross from the floor, and wrapped them in a pile of clothes she was taking to Goodwill. I curled into a ball and let the ache finish flowing.

When I finally went downstairs, Dad was sitting in his recliner with a bowl of chips and watching a re-run of *Adam-12*. Pete Malloy was mentoring Jim Reed in their black and white patrol car when a call came in about a hit and run. Dad was learning LA police jargon on a Sunday. He was relaxed, unpressured, and possibly as inspired as he could ever get, but still free. Mother was in the kitchen skinning potatoes, hammering steak, and making a loaf of bread. Her armpits were soaked.

"What's for dinner," I asked.

"Stewed beef," she said.

I studied her hands as they pumped the dough, dusted it with flour, and slammed a fist on its fullness. A teenage girl probably shouldn't give up on her mother, but sometimes there's no other way. I knew she would never be on my side.

I was in my senior year of high school when I heard the news about Father Daniel. At the kitchen table, Dad's mother, Grandma Brennan, was visiting from South Carolina and consoling Mother, who was holding a crumpled up moist tissue. The skin below her nostrils was raw and a newspaper was wide open on the table. As I walked towards them, Grandma Brennan playfully winked at me and threw her thick forearm over the paper.

"Oh, never mind, Faye," Mother said. "She's going to know soon enough."

Grandma lifted her arm and there was a photo of Father Daniel with bold-lettering above that read, *Saint Peter's Priest Arrested in Drug Ring*. Mother bowed her head.

"He fell from Grace, Hanna," Grandma said. She never shared awful news without a smile.

"Wow, drugs," I said. "I thought he was pretty old."

"I once heard of a drug ring in a nursing home," Grandma said in her rich drawl. "So, this might be a trend with the elderly." Her smile was huge at that point.

I desperately tried not to look at Grandma again. "What kind of drugs?" I asked.

Mother pulled her head up like it weighed fifty pounds. "I don't know," she said. "I didn't even—"

"Cocaine!" Grandma screamed. "Ain't that something!"

Mother got up and went to the sink. I walked over and put my hand on her shoulder.

"I'm sorry about this," I said. "You've known him a long time."

We both looked out the window and not another word was spoken about him. Grandma made crab-cakes, fried okra, and cornbread that night. Dad came to the dinner table faster than a pitcher's curve ball. Mother had two, maybe three, bites.

Years later and well into the night, I am lying in bed and paging through the memories of Father Daniel visiting me in my room. I wonder whose hands now hold the Bible without a page and I can't help but feel a loss that I was never given a fair chance with it. Dad is quietly in his nursing home chair six states over from me. Mother has gone to the ground. She was adamant in writing that her cross remain around her skeleton neck, and I would bet my favorite shirt on a hangar that there is mischievous black worm wrapped around it.

In the background of my closed eyes, I lead myself into an image of Father Daniel in jail. He is still as slimy as an industrial sized jug of vegetable oil. I imagine him counseling murderers and rapist on the importance of Atonement as he draws the sign of the cross into prison air before meals. Then I fantasize about visiting him where smudged glass from desperate lips separate us. I laugh deeply in front of him at the irony of trading an orange car for an orange jumpsuit. I allow him to scan me, so he can figure out for himself that I am not a whore. Then I say, "I guess life isn't going to work out for you," and before he can respond I open my eyes so I can return to the secure darkness and sound of God's crickets.

About the author:

Carol Cooley's short stories and essays have been published in numerous collections and magazines, including anthologies by *Creative Nonfiction*, *SUNY Press*, and *New Rivers Press*. She has received Honorable Mentions from the *North Carolina Literary Review* and *Glimmer Train Press*, and was awarded a writing fellowship to the Virginia Center for the Creative Arts. Carol lives in Wake Forest, North Carolina surrounded by nature and animals, where she can be found working on her debut novel. When Carol isn't writing, she spends her time advocating for quality eldercare and running around with her family and friends.

STAGE STRUCK
©2019 by Colin Brezicki

Gazing out from a bare stage at the rows of empty seats, she embraced the silence like a lost friend.

She felt weightless, suspended between two worlds.

The play was behind her, props and furniture already cleared, the painted flats in storage. Downstairs in wardrobe the costumes hung on racks, like dead souls.

What lay ahead had not begun, and the nothingness between felt precious.

Her moment over, she took a last look around the vacant auditorium and stepped off the stage.

She would drive by Alan's house on her way home. Seeing where he lived would reassure her he was real, and that they had happened.

I miss you already, Celia. The last thing he said to her before leaving for the airport. Now it sounded like a line from another play, and she wished he'd said something different.

The lobby was empty, as she hoped it would be. She must make a proper exit this time—after a positively last appearance—and she wanted the moment to herself. Ten years ago, she left the stage on a gurney, more embarrassed than frightened by her stroke. "I'm so sorry," she kept saying to everyone, like she had somehow intended to steal the show.

She later joked to Dr. Mitra, when he told her the partial paralysis on her left side was only temporary, that it must have been *a stroke of luck.*

But impaired memory put an end to her career. Or so she thought at the time.

It was Jasmine who'd shown her the ad, and she remembered laughing when she read it.

Auditions for the Niagara Amateur Players Society (NAPS) production of Noel Coward's "Hay Fever." Experience not essential.

"*NAPS*, Jasmine? Seriously? Grey heads nodding off in a matinée?"

"You owe it to yourself, Celia. You'll bag the lead for sure. And you'll meet people. Maybe a decent man, finally."

"You forget I have Alfie—he's decent enough. He's low-maintenance and house-trained, and he adores me."

"He's a cat."

"Exactly. What more do I need? I don't even have to walk him."

But she already knew *Hay Fever*, and the part of Judith Bliss appealed to her—another free spirit who resisted convention, Judith had also withdrawn to the country after a life in the theatre.

Trevor Bristow was ecstatic when she showed up for audition. "Celia Renfrew, my God. Wherever did you disappear to? Tell me you'll be Judith. Please!"

Her audition over, she told him she'd help out in any way, but asked that he not disclose her history to the cast.

It felt good to be involved again. A decade on her own had narrowed her life more than she realized.

And Alan Marchpane seemed, from all angles, to be a very decent man.

He admitted, when they knew each other better, to feeling intimidated by her at first. "I'm afraid your Judith Bliss knocked my old Richard Greatham sideways."

"She's supposed to. But I never realized she was making *you* flustered." Only a white lie.

She especially enjoyed their sofa scene, the eccentric leading lady flirting with the retired diplomat she'd invited down for the weekend. It allowed Celia to pretend she was desirable again.

And it gave their director something to feel excited about. "I'm *so* into this, you guys. Celia, you are *utterly* wicked. I love it."

Once, getting up from the sofa she carelessly brushed a hand across Richard Greatham's lap, and felt something *utterly* firm. She suppressed a giggle, but not the faint tingle of excitement.

She thought she'd got used to life without men.

"Bright blue eyes—Paul Newman eyes—and thick white hair, like someone gone into shock."

Jasmine laughed. "A *shock* of white hair, Celia? Too funny. What did he do in his other life?"

"I know nothing except he's English and shy, and he gets aroused in our couch scene."

She laughed again. "He'll ask you out, I know it."

It came out of nowhere.

She was driving him home on a night that turned wet and windy, and they were discussing an incident at rehearsal.

Trevor's improv games were not going down well with the cast and Celia had already apprised him of their unease. "They just want the director to tell them where to stand and when to speak."

Trevor shook his head. "They aren't *seeing* each other. They're acting, not *being*."

That evening he had wanted them to play Bus Stop, so they could become more aware of other people. "We need to be *real*." He explained the improv. "You enter the space when you feel like it. You can sit on the bench or just stand, but however you do it, you wait for the bus. You don't acknowledge anyone else because you're all strangers. You look to see if the bus is coming. You check your watch. You stare into space. Be aware of people but don't acknowledge them. Let everything evolve until someone *has* to speak. Speaking ends the scene. But it can take a while if you don't force it. No mugging."

Angela Parton spoke. "So, you want us to stand at a bus stop with other people and pretend to be real."

"No. You *are* real. No pretending, no acting. It's truth we want here."

"Got it." She marched into the middle of the circle and sat down on the bench. After a moment she leaned forward to look for the bus, then took out her cell phone.

Jack Mallory sauntered in, stood a few feet away and took out *his* phone.

Trevor exploded. "No phones! Come *on*, people. How can you be aware of each other when you're staring into your *phones*?"

Cynthia Flowers, who never said anything, pitched in. "But it's what everyone does. You said you wanted real."

A discussion ensued about what was real and what wasn't until Trevor took over. "Okay, it's a *dead* zone. There's no signal, so your phones can't work."

Phil Broadhurst walked into the space and sat on the bench. Celia followed him after a moment. She stood to one side and took out her phone, intending only to wave it around for a signal, before putting it away again. But Phil intervened.

"Dead zone," he announced, ending the scene before it got started.

Trevor gave an audible sigh and announced a short break before they got on with Act Two.

In the car afterwards, Alan remarked that Trevor's improvs reminded him of the silly parlor games the mad Bliss family imposed on their bemused houseguests in the play.

She laughed. "Don't ever tell *him* that."

"It's annoying, all this stuff about finding our *core* and dredging up our personal memories. What's it in aid of?" His voice had an edge now.

"It's called the Method and it trains actors to not look at each other while they mumble their lines to themselves." She laughed. "The odd thing is that the Bliss family never mean a word they say to *anyone*. They pretend all the time."

"So, does the one cancel out the other?"

"What do you mean?"

"Well, if you want to be one of the Blisses, and all they ever do is act a part, then why not just act the part and not worry about being real? You can only be them if you're pretending, right?" He pointed at a driveway ahead. "It's this one."

She checked her mirror. "Don't tell Trevor that either, or you'll upset him. Remember, he thinks you're one of the good ones."

"Good at acting, or at being real?"

"Which do you do better?" She meant it to be a Judith line, not her own, but it unsettled him.

"What's that supposed to mean?"

"Nothing. It just came out—something Judith would say." She felt the awkwardness between them as she pulled up to his garage and switched off the engine. "I didn't mean anything by it, Alan, I promise."

He looked away for a moment. "I overreacted. Sorry. I shouldn't be so sensitive."

She seized on a line from the play. *"There you are, you see. Saying the right thing. You always say the right thing and no one ever knows what you're thinking."*

He laughed, then went quiet. "So, I'll tell you what I'm thinking. I'd like to have lunch with you sometime."

"Why?" She said it *without* thinking.

He seemed unfazed. "Because I get hungry at lunchtime." He smiled. "If we find we have nothing to talk about, we can run lines."

She couldn't decline. Not now—nor did she want to. "I'd like that. But we go Dutch."

"As you wish."

Jasmine was delighted to hear it. "I won't say I told you so."

He was already seated at a window table when she arrived. He stood to pull out a chair for her, then handed her coat to the waiter. "Just got here myself." He smiled. "We beat the storm."

"I didn't realize one was coming." The morning was cold but bright when she decided to walk to the restaurant, though the sky had clouded over on the way. If the weather turned nasty, she'd ask him to drop her off.

He looked smart in his cardigan, button-down shirt, pressed slacks and winter brogues. She felt a flutter of anticipation as she sat. "Thank you." It had been a while.

Their table overlooked the park. A light snow had begun. On the sidewalk across the road a woman in a leather coat stopped to let her white poodle squat to do its business. Celia glanced at Alan when the woman reached into her pocket for the little blue bag.

He smiled. "How about an appetizer?"

She laughed. "Not something I could do." When he raised an eyebrow she quickly added, "I mean—*that*," and wiggled her fingers in a mimed plastic bag. "It's why I have a cat."

"Alfie. I remember."

"You should remember your lines so well." She needed another excuse to laugh. "Kidding."

"I made a career of it."

"What, kidding or remembering lines?"

He looked blank for a second. "No idea why I said that. Never mind. Shall we have wine?" He handed her the list. "You choose. Whatever you like." He opened a menu.

She chose the chardonnay and asked for an ice bucket. She wasn't used to drinking wine at lunch but this was an occasion.

He asked how she was managing, working with amateurs, and she said she liked their attitude. "And Trevor got the message about his improv games." She smiled. "Now, tell me about you. What did you do that made you have to remember lines?"

"Just another kind of acting." But he didn't elaborate; instead he went on to précis his past like it was something to be got out of the way. He lost his wife to leukemia only two years earlier. His son, a chartered accountant, lived in England. He visited his grandchildren in London twice a year, and every second visit he hopped across to Luxembourg to see friends he used to work with.

She wondered if losing his wife had made his hair turn prematurely white. Grief could do that.

"Did *you* ever marry?" His question came out of the blue. "Sorry. It's not my business, really."

She didn't mind. "I came close once, in my thirties, but he turned out not to be the man I thought he was. Or maybe I wasn't the woman he imagined me to be. Either way, it didn't happen."

"Can I ask why you left the stage?"

She smiled. "I had a stroke. Transient ischaemic attack—right in the middle of a performance. A show-stopper, you might say."

He smiled. "So, tell me."

"Arms and the Man. Mrs. Petkoff had just told her daughter's unsuitable suitor he must 'leave the house at once' when she suddenly felt very odd—a tingling down her left side, and her mind a blank. So, it was Mrs. Petkoff who had to leave the house at once—in an ambulance."

"That's awful. I'm so sorry." He shrugged. "But you seem all right now."

"No lasting damage, thank God."

"And you never went back? I mean, until now?"

"Oh, they told me I could once they got my meds right. But I lost my nerve. I became paranoid about forgetting lines."

"And now?"

"It's been okay, and we're in the home stretch."

He nodded. "Well, you've been an inspiration to all of us."

It sounded pat. Something said at a Rotary gathering or an awards ceremony. But maybe she was being too critical. He had paid her a compliment. "I like to be supportive."

Their meal arrived—she had ordered the crab salad, he the linguini—and they began eating. She commented on the food, and he remarked on the wine, and each said in turn how lovely it all was, until she felt the conversation needed a reboot. She reached across and touched his sleeve. *"Oh, do stop being so non-committal, Richard. It's doubly annoying in the face of my having said so much about myself."*

He laughed and gave his scripted reply. *"I never realize how dead I am until I meet people like you."*

"*I don't think you're the least bit dead.*" She smiled. "And now you must tell me about the rest of you. What did you do in Luxembourg?"

"I connected people with other people," he said. "Not very exciting, I'm afraid." He paused. "Do you know what a möbius is?"

"Amoebas?"

He shook his head. "Möbius."

"No idea."

"Think of a fan belt in a figure eight. It connects two engine parts and runs between them." He shrugged. "That was me. I connected people who needed each other."

She took out her phone and tapped in the letters. A picture came up of a slowly revolving figure eight, its inside twisting into its outside as it turned. She angled the screen so he could see. "Hard to follow which side is up."

He nodded. "Part of its charm. I once lined up its manufacturer with several companies that had a use for it. So, I'm familiar with how it works."

"Did you make masses of money being a—" she glanced at her phone "—möbius yourself?"

He shook his head. "Not right away. Eventually, I did okay connecting corporations with the bureaucrats in Brussels. After our son left home, Gloria became an administrator at the American school. We did well enough, but then she became ill and wanted to return to Canada. We lived in Toronto for two years, and when she died, I moved down here." He went quiet again.

Another awkward spin out. She tried again. "Did you act before? I think you're very good."

He waved it off. "I was in the drama club at my school." He smiled. "It was good training."

"For what?"

"For my career. Finding an *A* that needed a *B*, and vice versa, then putting them together."

She thought for a moment. "How does theatre prepare you for that?"

"A play needs an audience; an audience needs a play. The actor connects them. Isn't that how it works?"

"I suppose." She thought of being a character onstage herself—Judith Bliss, say—and not being sure which side was up. Had she really spent a whole career not knowing if she was herself or someone else? The thought was unsettling.

"A penny for them," he said after a moment.

"My father would say that."

He nodded. "Mine too."

"Maybe everyone did back then."

"Maybe they did."

"So, are we doing Pinter now?"

He smiled and looked out the window. It had begun to snow more heavily, lazy, thick flakes tumbling out of a charcoal sky. "We did Pinter at A-level. *The Birthday Party*. Not a happy play, I remember."

"Where were you at school?"

"Cranleigh. A boarding school in Surrey. From when I was eight."

"Good God, what was that like? Isn't eight kind of young to be sent away?"

"I got used to it." He gazed out at the snow. "Funny. Whenever I went home for vacation, I felt I was only visiting. Like home was a place to kill time between terms." He seemed to be searching for the right words. He put down his fork and dabbed the sides of his mouth with his napkin. "Anyway, I loved being in the plays at school. Silly Victorian melodramas, mostly—it was an all-boys back then, so the younger pupils played the female roles."

"And you learned your lines before anyone else, I bet."

He nodded and looked at her. "I was good at doing whatever people asked me to."

It sounded complicit, the way he said it. It seemed now that the conversation had shifted to the edge of something daring and he was inviting her to share it with him.

She sipped her coffee as she looked at him. The silence wasn't uncomfortable now at least. She felt his separation, and her own, like a teller's window between them. She watched her hand move across the silence and under the glass to touch his. "Are we being us now, do you think?" This wasn't a Judith line.

He looked at her and smiled. "I hope so." He gave her hand a squeeze then let go. "Tell me, what was home like for you?"

She withdrew her hand. "It was a place where I always imagined being somewhere else. A bit like you." She hadn't thought about it that way until now. "My parents didn't show much emotion, even my mother was a closed book; so I grew up believing that's how I should behave. School was tedious, mostly. I lived for summers at our cottage in Algonquin. I would wander the woods and canoe on the lake, talking to myself."

"Really?"

She laughed. "It sounds weird, but I did. I imagined people out of books I'd read—*Black Beauty, A Wizard of Earthsea, The Secret Garden*—and I spoke to them. We'd have real conversations."

"Ever the actor, then."

She laughed. "I shocked my parents when I applied to theatre school. They had no idea."

"You should have played Bus Stop with them."

"Why?"

He smiled. "So, they could *really see you*, as our director would say."

She nodded. "Quite. But they never did. I found people at theatre school more real and alive than anyone I'd known."

The wine had gone to her head, but she didn't care. They were sharing something from their lives now. Paying attention. And with the snow thickening outside the window he spoke the words she wanted to hear.

"Can I drive you home?"

"I'd like that, thank you."

It was all so easy, like following a script. She let him undress her and felt his smooth skin against hers. She felt his breath catch when she touched him, and her own when he entered her.

Afterwards, and absurdly for a moment, she forgot his name. Lost in the pleasure, in the warmth of his body, the smoothness of his skin against hers. Alan. Of course.

He stroked her hair.

Later, they awoke to a scratching at her door. She turned and kissed him on the cheek. "Alfie's not used to someone being in my bedroom. What should we do about that?"

He smiled. "Let him get used to it?"

She kissed him and felt his arousal. "I can see you're game."

They were together most evenings after rehearsal. He felt more comfortable staying at her place because she lived along the parkway where trees and shrubbery separated the snow-filled lawns. His house in town was part of a terrace, and neighbors tended to mind everyone's business, he said. She was happy to have him, and Alfie got used to his presence.

On rehearsal-free Sundays, weather permitting, they would go for long drives. To Burlington once to see a matinée. Another time she showed him her old neighborhood in Toronto, but the house was long gone, replaced by a more elaborate home with a pool. She wondered if he might want to show her where he and his wife had lived, but he didn't suggest it. Too painful, she thought. He said he'd like to visit Algonquin with her in the spring. He'd never been, he said.

Jasmine gave her space. "You can introduce me when you're ready." Once, when she came for tea, she asked if Celia thought she and Alan might live together one day.

"We haven't discussed it so far. I'd consider it, though."

"You don't have to fall in love, my dear, not at our stage. You only need to make each other happy, and that seems to be happening."

Love wasn't a feeling she was familiar with. Not since Gerry, all those years ago, and that hadn't lasted. Alan must have loved his wife, she thought, though he didn't mention her now. In time she would ask him more about her—Gloria—so he would know she felt comfortable hearing about her.

"Do you think it's odd we haven't said 'I love you'?" She asked him one evening in bed.

"I haven't thought about it."

"About whether you love me?"

"About our not saying it. Maybe at our age people don't fall head over heels." He laughed. "We find it harder to get back up again."

"You don't want to risk it, you mean?"

He kissed her hair. "I'm very fond of you, Celia. And you make me happy."

She turned over to face him. "And you make me happy."

"Then maybe for people our age it's the same thing." He slid his hand between her thighs.

"You've taken your little pill, haven't you?"

Later, as she lay awake and listened to him breathing softly beside her, she thought she might be in love with him.

They had said their goodbyes the day of the cast party, before he left for Toronto. He was staying the night at an airport hotel and catching his flight in the morning.

I miss you already, Celia.

Jasmine was her guest at the party. She had helped with makeup and stayed on to see some of the performances. Having finally met Alan, she had approved. "He's lovely, and I'm not surprised you're besotted." One morning, when they were on the phone, she said she'd looked him up on the web. "All I found was *marchpane*. Did you know it's a confection? Sort of like marzipan." She laughed. "No wonder he's such a sweetie."

She'd never thought of looking him up. It would be like going behind his back. He had told her who he was, and she was glad Jasmine found nothing in her search. *Besotted* was appropriate, though. Besotted was like being in love. At the party she felt an ache whenever his name was mentioned.

"What a surprise Alan Marchpane turned out to be."

Driving home from the theatre the next morning after her moment alone on the empty stage, she remembered to go past his house. Turning into his street and approaching his place she spotted an unfamiliar car in the driveway. A woman stood on the porch. She seemed to be fiddling with the front door.

Celia pulled up at the curb and lowered her window. "Can I help you with something?"

The woman turned and peered across the lawn at her, squinting in the sun. "I'm sorry. Do we know each other?"

She got out of her car and walked up the driveway. "I'm Celia Renfrew. A friend of Alan's."

The woman smiled and came down the steps. "How do you do. I'm his house agent, Jennifer Bream. I'm just installing the lock box now." She pointed at the bulky device attached to the door handle. "I'm with Palmer and Tarrant." She looked at Celia again. "I've seen you before, haven't I?"

"I don't think so." She could feel a pit in her stomach.

"The play. You were in the play. I came on opening night. Oh my God, you were hilarious." She stretched the word out like she was reliving the hilarity.

"Thank you. Alan's selling his house?" Had they talked of him moving in with her when he returned from London? Or was it a conversation she had with herself?

"What goes round comes round. I sold him this house when he moved here from Ottawa." She touched her arm. "Are you okay?"

"Yes, I'm sorry. I'm in a muddle." Ottawa? He told her Toronto. "I didn't realize he was selling so soon." She took a deep breath.

"He signed last week. There's a lot to do. The furniture is going into storage once the house is sold."

"Of course." She began to feel nauseous.

"Are you sure you're alright?" The woman took her arm. "You've gone pale."

"I have to sit down." Her own voice sounded far away.

"Come into the house. Don't worry about your boots." She removed the lock box and led her through the hall into the living room. She took her coat and eased her onto the sofa. "You sit there and put your head down to your knees. Like that. I'll get some water. Just stay like that."

She heard her go out of the room and then a tap running.

When she returned, Celia sat back and accepted the glass of water.

"Just sip it, don't gulp it."

She felt her pulse racing, a pounding in her ears. After a while it eased. "Thank you. I've no idea what that was."

The woman spoke quietly. "More water? No? Okay. I'm just going out to the car for a second. Don't stand up or do anything quickly. I'll be right back."

"Thank you." She began to look around the room. So elegantly furnished.

But there was something odd. It was like a showroom. The shelves displayed rows of faux leather, gold-tooled volumes—mail-order collections of unread books to fill a space. Same with the Dutch figures and porcelain vases. The framed paintings were just more interior design. A seascape. Something else in pastels. A bowl of bright fruit. The floral arrangement on the glass table was silk. There were no photos.

When the woman came back and asked how she was doing, she forced a nod. "Has he already taken his personal things? I mean, photos, that sort of thing?"

She shook her head. "Not that I know. It's an agent's dream, this house. Everything in its place and ready to view." She sat down beside her. "Are you sure you're feeling better?"

She looked at her and nodded again. She felt she must be disappearing because the woman seemed to be staring through her at the wall behind. Her arms and legs didn't feel part of her anymore. The room had gone blurry, like it was beaming up to somewhere else.

She as well—into the vacant space between everything else. The woman's voice reverberated for a moment, then disappeared into the palpable silence.

About the author:

Colin turned to writing after a teaching life in England and Canada. He has published two novels, "A Case for Dr. Palindrome", and "All That Remains" (recently a finalist in the Tucson Book Festival). His short fiction includes winners of the J.K. Galbraith Fiction Award, the Literal Latté (New York) fiction contest, Bosque fiction contest (New Mexico), Canadian Authors' Ten Stories High, and a finalist in the Writers Union of Canada fiction contest. He has published in academic and literary journals and the "Globe and Mail," and he's a regular Column Six contributor to the "Voice of Pelham."

53487995R00086

Made in the USA
Middletown, DE
12 July 2019